W9-BHH-077

Lisa had never known any man like Zander

He was like a rock that gave out the heat of that day's sun for a long time after the sun had set.

As he came toward her, Lisa could feel his power, the waves of strength emanating from him. He smiled down at her, and Lisa's tremulous greeting gave away her pleasure.

Zander opened his arms, and she went to him. She laughed happily.

His lips briefly touched hers. When he lifted his head, he remarked, "I had to catch that smile of yours. I'll wrap it securely around my heart."

"And keep it there forever?" Lisa asked shyly.

"Forever," he replied.

Books by Lilian Peake

HARLEQUIN ROMANCES
1674 – MAN OUT OF REACH
1700 – GONE BEFORE MORNING
1726 – MAN IN CHARGE
1778 – A SENSE OF BELONGING
1831 – MASTER OF THE HOUSE
1855 – THE IMPOSSIBLE MARRIAGE
1868 – THE DREAM ON THE HILL
1900 – MOONRISE OVER THE MOUNTAINS
1944 – HEART IN THE SUNLIGHT
2220 – REBEL IN LOVE
2279 – STRANGER ON THE BEACH
2404 – PROMISE AT MIDNIGHT
2603 – NIGHT OF POSSESSION

HARLEQUIN PRESENTS
198 – NO FRIEND OF MINE
206 – THE LITTLE IMPOSTOR
213 – SOMEWHERE TO LAY MY HEAD
225 – A GIRL ALONE
229 – PASSIONATE INVOLVEMENT
316 – NO SECOND PARTING
330 – ENEMY FROM THE PAST
341 – RUN FOR YOUR LOVE
353 – DANGEROUS DECEPTION
384 – A RING FOR A FORTUNE
407 – A SECRET AFFAIR
424 – GREGG BARRATT'S WOMAN
454 – STRANGERS INTO LOVERS
474 – ACROSS A CROWDED ROOM
496 – DAY OF POSSESSION
524 – BITTER REVENGE
612 – PASSIONATE INTRUDER

These books may be available at your local bookseller.

For a free catalog listing all titles currently available,
send your name and address to:

Harlequin Reader Service
P.O. Box 52040, Phoenix, AZ 85072-9988
Canadian address: Stratford, Ontario N5A 6W2

Night of Possession

Lilian Peake

Harlequin Books

TORONTO • NEW YORK • LONDON
AMSTERDAM • PARIS • SYDNEY • HAMBURG
STOCKHOLM • ATHENS • TOKYO • MILAN

Original hardcover edition published in 1983
by Mills & Boon Limited

ISBN 0-373-02603-X

Harlequin Romance first edition February 1984

CHAPTER ONE

EVEN as Lisa looked across the hotel lounge and searched for her friends, she was conscious of being watched. Instead of turning to trace the silent yet strangely magnetic source of power, she continued to seek out the two familiar faces among the many tourists.

Her friends were not there. Although they had told her to wait in the bar, she would have to move, if only to get away from—whom? Her head turned. Instinct had taken over from reason and compelled her to look for the presence—she could think of no better word, since the feeling of being concentrated upon was so uncanny—which was continuing to menace her from behind.

Her first impression of the person whose scrutiny had acted so effectively on her nervous system was that he was bearded, tall and had a slightly longer than usual hairstyle. There was a certain quality in his assessing glance that had her heart stumbling with annoyance.

Her dress was of cream silk, the skirt soft and floating. A collar framed her oval-shaped face, while the short sleeves revealed arms which had not yet had time to acquire the tan that covered the man's hands, neck and face.

Lisa threw him a look which, she hoped, would freeze his blood. His answer was to form his mouth into a smile, take a drink from the glass he held as he rested sideways against the bar, and watch her over its rim.

With a swing of her rustling skirt, she withdrew her cold stare and looked with something near to desperation over her shoulder. Would Myra and Phil never come? Turning from the archway, Lisa retraced her steps and made her way back to the entrance foyer.

There were people on the curving staircase, and the lift was emptying itself, but there was still no sign of her friends. Having arranged to meet them in the lounge-bar, she was forced to return to that particular place. If that staring stranger was still there, she would walk quickly past, averting her head.

The black-haired stranger had not moved. A curious panic had Lisa searching for a seat. There was an empty three-seater couch set at right angles to the floor-to-ceiling windows. She walked across to it with as much grace as her muted panic would allow.

Settling into it, she divided her time between gazing through the archway for her friends and staring out at the distant mountains. Beyond the hotel's boundaries lay a strange and fascinating world. Bringing her gaze nearer, she studied the white modern villas and apartments stretching uphill and into the near distance.

There was a movement opposite and she turned with a bright smile to greet her companions. It was not the face of a friend that returned her look. The long-limbed figure of the stranger was indolently stretched across from her, his sandalled feet pushed under the glass-topped table between them.

Still he stared, head back and at rest, arms folded lightly across the partially unfastened white shirt. His jeans were taut across his lean hips. His eyelids drooped to hide his opinion of the assets of the girl he studied so closely.

He had every right, Lisa told herself, to be where he was. Nor was there any law to prevent him from conducting his scrutiny—except, she thought angrily, an unwritten social law which taught that to stare was not only rude, but a kind of invasion of a person's—this person's—privacy.

Stretching forward to the table, she took up a magazine and flicked the glossy pages, only to discover that it was printed in Spanish. Her knowledge of the language being no better than phrase-book level, she replaced it hurriedly, lifting her eyes in a swift, I-dare-you-to-laugh glance at her irritating fellow-tourist.

His eyes, however, had not wavered from her face. Even if he had laughed, he could not have brought such a flare of colour to her cheeks. Grasping another glossy magazine, having made sure first that it was printed in English, she endeavoured to lose herself in its contents.

Her eyes did her mind's bidding, but it was her concentration that let her down. She could not control its wanderings, nor curiously did she really want to. Her hands lowered the magazine sufficiently for her eyes to stare over the top.

It was safe, she discovered, to study him since he had taken the magazine she had discarded and was reading it as if he were born to speak the language. Maybe he was. The thought had not occurred to her until now, yet . . . yet there was something about him that nagged at her memory. Had she seen him somewhere before? Under that beard, was there a face she knew? It was his eyes that troubled her, and which, she was certain, held the key. The key to what?

The moment she found herself staring into a pair of quizzical brown eyes, she lowered her own, but not before she saw the laughter lines crinkle and ray outward in an unspoken mockery at her wary curiosity about him.

Her interest was captured at last by a story in the magazine. When her friends called, 'Hey, Lisa, descend from those heights and join us!' she jerked with surprise.

Moving along the seat to give her friends more room, she put aside the magazine, registering that the darkly-bearded man had also dispensed with his reading matter. His head turned from contemplating the scenery outside to watching with undisguised interest the arrival of the newcomers.

Myra and Phil were holding hands. When they were comfortably seated, Phil's arm went round Myra's waist. They had been married for five weeks, yet it was plain by the way Myra played with the gold band on her wedding finger that it still felt new.

Five months ago, Lisa and her current boy-friend had arranged to take their holiday with Myra and Phil. When Lisa broke with Don, her boy-friend, his booking had been cancelled.

'Three's not company,' Lisa had said at the time. 'I'll cancel, too.'

Myra, who worked for the same construction company as she did, had told her, 'If you cancel, Phil and I will, too. You wouldn't want to ruin our holiday for us, now, would you?'

To complicate matters, they had decided suddenly to get married. Since their holidays had already been paid for, Lisa's offer once again to cancel her booking had, as they had all known, been merely a gesture.

'By then,' Phil had reassured Lisa, with a grin at his wife-to-be, 'Myra and I will be an old married couple. Having you with us will relieve the boredom which will have set in!'

Looking at the radiance of their faces as they sat beside her now, Lisa knew that five weeks of marriage had made them even more in love.

Phil leaned forward and spoke across his wife. 'Sorry we were so long changing after our swim, Lisa,' he said. He grinned at Myra. 'You know how it is with women—can't decide which dress to wear.'

'How can you say that,' Myra protested, 'when it was you who delayed me!'

Phil lifted a shoulder, still grinning. 'You know how it is.'

Lisa smiled back. 'I'll take a guess.' She inspected her friend's choice of outfit. 'You look good, Myra. I was with you when you bought that dress, wasn't I? In Oxford Street one lunchtime?'

Myra nodded a little absently. Lisa followed her eyes, only to colour deeply when she found that the hotel guest with the dark beard and even darker hair had not removed his gaze from her, despite her friends' arrival.

Myra turned a look of puzzlement towards Lisa, who pressed her lips together in an effort to convey to her friend just how angry she was at the man's insolence. Myra whispered in her ear, 'Want to move?'

Lisa was about to agree when the man stood, nodded at Myra and Phil and walked slowly away. Lisa caught herself watching the fluid movement of his limbs, then reproached her thoughts for their waywardness.

'What was that all about?' Myra enquired, looking after him. 'Got yourself a new boy-friend?'

'I haven't exchanged a single word with the man,' Lisa exclaimed. 'All he's done since I arrived down here is stare at me as if I were a picture on the wall—and with about as much feeling! He's embarrassed me so much I——'

'He fancies you,' Phil offered, smiling. 'If I weren't an old married man, I'd fancy you myself.' At which bold statement, his wife reached up and pulled his hair.

Making their way towards the restaurant for dinner, Lisa found herself looking at the staircase and watching the arrival of the lifts. She told herself it was a purely defensive action, since she sensed that the man was a threat. The thought was not followed up by the question, a threat to what?

Exotic plants decorated the foyer through which they passed. The hotel's décor had plainly been designed to live up to the image expected of the luxury hotel that it was. Myra led the way to their usual table by the window, where floor-length curtains billowed in the cooling breeze.

Lisa, who faced the restaurant entrance, half listened to her friends' chatter, laughing in the right places, hoping they would not notice how her gaze kept straying as each new guest entered the large, busy room.

The man for whom she was looking did not enter alone. In common with his three male companions, he was dressed more formally. His suit was of cream linen, while his dark brown shirt was open at the neck. Lisa found herself staring in an effort to find, beneath this fresh aspect of the stranger's personality, the lustful male who had earlier eyed her so uninhibitedly, but there seemed to be not even a sign of him.

A swift glance around the restaurant seemed to tell the man all he appeared to want to know. His eyes passed over Lisa as if she were just another tree in a forest full of trees. His seeming non-recognition of the girl at whom he had stared long enough surely to recall her every feature irritated Lisa intensely. This, in turn, caused her to be angry with herself for attaching so much importance to the whole episode.

In one thing she might, she conceded, have been

mistaken. Since he was dining with a group of men, whose manner, like his, seemed to be so businesslike as to dismiss the whole world of tourism as a nuisance only just to be tolerated, Lisa decided that he was not a holidaymaker as she had assumed.

Tearing her mind from the man, she tuned in to her friends' conversation. From their absorption in each other, it seemed she had not been missed.

There was a pause in their conversation. Lisa asked, as they awaited the arrival of the dessert, 'What's on the menu for this evening?'

'We've been arguing about that,' Myra answered. 'I want to read in the main lounge.'

'And I,' her husband added, 'want to dance. Come on,' his thin face broadened into a smile, 'see it my way. You can read any old time.'

'You mean let you have your own way again,' retorted Myra, pushing back her pale brown hair. She sighed. 'Just this once, then.' Turning to Lisa, she informed her, 'We dance. But I must go and change.'

Phil groaned. 'Not again?'

'Why do you think I brought all those dresses, if not to wear them?'

Phil pushed away his dessert dish. 'Okay, I know when I'm beaten.'

Myra's hand came out to stroke his hair. 'I only want to make myself look beautiful for you, darling.'

He smiled at his wife, then said to Lisa, 'You know when she's most beautiful, don't you?'

'Phil!' Myra exclaimed, pretending to be horrified.

Lisa laughed, her head going back, her deep brown hair swinging with the movement. Her eyes twinkled as she answered, with mock earnestness, 'No, I don't Phil. Tell me.'

Phil returned her glance with just a touch of embarrassment, then produced his wide smile. 'Come on, Myra. You two women—you're henpecking me! Lisa, see you in the ballroom.' Another glance at his wife, then he added, 'In about two hours from now.'

'Thirty minutes, Lisa,' Myra promised. 'If the dancing hasn't started by then, we'll have a drink. Grab a table in a corner if you beat us to it.'

Lisa left them as the lift reached the second floor. Next floor up was another restaurant and a covered balcony. The room which Lisa occupied opened out on to a balcony overlooking the sea.

Knowing it would not take her half an hour to change, she wandered outside to stare down at the rocks among which grew strange plants, a spreading bed of tiny flowers, shrubs with long and pointed leaves among numerous cacti. Here and there, a palm tree waved in the constant breeze that cooled the overheated air.

The dress she wore was a mixture of colours. It was silky and calf-length, with narrow shoulder straps which made her wish that their two days spent sunbathing on the private beach adjacent to the hotel had given her white skin more than a mere hint of tan. Her white choker necklace matched her sandals and her clutch-bag. Her hair was brushed softly and thickly into tapered curls.

Sighing at her own reflection, she wondered why she was bothering to take such care with her appearance. I'm the odd one out, she thought, not with self-pity but with a sense of regret for her companions' sakes. In spite of their repeated denials, she knew she must be something of a liability to them.

A glance at her watch told her that the half-hour which Myra had estimated it would take her to change had passed. Her hope that she would find them there at a table waiting for her was, as she had dreaded, unfulfilled. Always she was first, no matter where the meeting place might be.

Over the past two or so days, she had grown accustomed to her lonely wait. Tonight, for some reason she could not immediately understand, the thought of those minutes of waiting filled her with alarm.

Standing in the arched entrance to the ballroom, she let her eyes sweep the tables, many of which were occupied. There were, to her relief, a few unclaimed near to darker corners.

As she made for one of them, her glance was caught by a group of men at the bar across the circular expanse of the dancing area. There were four of them, one of whom stood out from the rest through his extra height, his cream linen suit—but most of all his dark beard.

Seating herself at the table for four, Lisa busied herself with the contents of her bag, rearranging her choker beads and smoothing her hair. Only when she had exhausted every possible reason for not looking around her did she lift her head and stare across at the bar.

Her hope that the men had gone was not fulfilled. They were there, the four of them, but only one was gazing her way. Embarrassed, she turned her head, silently begging her friends to appear and release her from this awful feeling of isolation amongst a crowd of complete strangers.

Her eyes were drawn back to the group. Yes, they were all looking at her now. The bearded man spoke and his companions turned their heads to listen. Lisa saw his hand move with a touch of dismissal. He was still speaking and they nodded. Was he belittling her to them? Was that the reason for their smiles? Lisa felt her cheeks grow warm. If they were laughing at her for being alone . . .

When she saw him making his way towards her, she half rose, ready for flight. Realising how unsophisticated such an action must look to this man with the knowing eyes and faintly cynical smile, Lisa sank back, clasped her hands and let her glance wander to the windows, seeking the view of the darkening sea beyond.

A scrape of chair jerked her from her false contemplation of the scenery. He was looking at her, eyebrows lifted in query.

'I'm sorry,' she told the man hastily, 'this table is already taken.'

'You're waiting for your friends?' His voice was low, his English eminently understandable. Plainly, she reflected, it was his native tongue, which answered the question of his origins. There were, however, many more unanswered questions about the man—why he

was here, for one thing, in this beautiful Canary Islands
territory, this place called Lanzarote whose landscape,
someone had said, resembled that of the moon.

There was another question, she thought, to which
she would never know the answer—why those other
three men had melted away as if at a command from
him. Yet they had been friends, hadn't they, equals,
even if they were here on a business project?

'I'm waiting for my friends,' she answered his
question, 'so I'm sorry, but this table will soon be
occupied.'

'You have two friends?' By now he was seated
opposite her. He pointed. 'But four chairs?'

'Two friends, but——' The afternoon's anger against
this audacious man had returned, and she responded
sharply, 'but we like being three. Not four,' she added
pointedly.

He smiled, leaning back and running a thoughtful
hand the length of his beard. 'But at the moment,
you're only one. Until your companions arrive you
wouldn't really mind, would you, if I kept you
company?'

How could she refuse, since he had every right to sit
where he was? Shaking her head rather than committing
herself by putting her answer into words, Lisa looked
with something like desperation towards the entrance.
Two by two, people entered, but every time it was the
wrong couple who came in.

'Can I get you a drink?' His question pulled her mind
back to his presence.

'No, thank you.' Her voice had been over-sharp, so
she softened her answer by adding, 'I'll wait until my
friends come. But please, have one yourself.'

He inclined his head with the merest hint of mockery,
raising his hand as a wine waiter passed nearby. The
stranger gave his order, speaking, to Lisa's surprise, in
fluent Spanish. Had she been wrong about his
nationality after all?

'Are you enjoying your vacation?' His query came
over the first sounds from the four-piece band as they
tuned their instruments.

'Yes. Well, I think I am.' Lisa rotated the small bowl of flowers which decorated the table. 'We've only been here two days.' Glancing at him, she found that his eyes were on her hands. At once she guessed he was searching for any rings of significance.

He dwelt thoughtfully upon her face. 'You only *think* you are? A case of two's company, three's a pain in the neck?'

Lisa laughed, her head going back. His gaze fixed on her features again. He was not laughing with her. A tingle of shock ran down her spine as she realised just how attractive he was. If only, she thought, I could really *see* his face, if only it were free of beard and moustache. Some woman, one day, would coax him into removing it all. The wish whipped through her mind that she could be that woman . . .

His drink was placed in front of him and he paid at once, with a tip that must have been generous by the smiling bow accorded him by the waiter.

'Three's a pain,' she agreed, studying the flowers again, 'but I keep it to myself.'

'There must be a reason,' he commented, taking a swallow from his glass.

Reluctantly, she enlightened him. 'I broke with my boy-friend. He cancelled his booking.'

The man's eyes narrowed momentarily, then he smiled, remarking, 'Which left you with a double room and only you to occupy it.'

The statement angered her. 'You've got it wrong! Try again, Mr . . . I'm sorry, I don't know your name.'

'Cameron, Zander Cameron. Before you ask, it's a shortened form of Alexander. You're Lisa—I heard your friends. Lisa what?'

'Maynard,' she answered shortly. So he thought he was making a holiday pick-up and, having no male escort, she would be ripe for pursuit by him? 'Is your wife with you, Mr Cameron? Or maybe your girl-friend?'

He smiled, as if guessing her intention of putting him down. 'No to both.'

Her eyes were drawn to the entrance. Phil was there, gesticulating. Zander Cameron followed her eyes.

'Please excuse me.' She rose and pushed her way through the crowds.

'Sorry, Lisa,' said Phil. 'We won't be joining you tonight.' His face was a little flushed. 'Do you mind?'

Lisa smiled understandingly. 'Forget about me, Phil—I'll be okay. I've got company. Uninvited guest, but in the circumstances, maybe a good thing.'

Phil stared. 'Isn't that the guy who couldn't keep his eyes off you earlier?' He saw Lisa's embarrassment. 'Well, anyway,' he concluded, 'you should be all right for this evening. Keep him guessing. And at arm's length!'

Lisa laughed. 'Advice from Uncle Phil! Okay, I know how to take care of myself.' But do I? she thought, remembering how hurt she had been at Don's announcement that he'd found someone else.

Phil was on his way. 'See you at breakfast,' he called.

Lisa, watching him go, felt overwhelmingly vulnerable. All around her were people laughing, talking, dancing. Odd one out again, she thought. I shouldn't have come. I might as well go upstairs, too. Feeling for her clutch-bag, she remembered where she had left it. Which meant she would have to return to the table after all.

'Friends not coming?' Zander Cameron asked, idly turning his glass.

'No.' She looked around. 'I only came back to collect my bag.' She frowned. 'That's odd—it's gone! I could have sworn——' She stared at the brown-eyed stranger. 'Did you see someone take it?'

He did not answer her question. He asked instead, 'Will you let me take your friends' place?'

It was her turn to sidetrack. 'I must find my bag. Please will you help me?' Her brow pleated, her blue eyes pleaded.

He smiled, seeming to enjoy her predicament. 'Answer my question first, then I'll answer yours.'

'Oh, yes, yes! Now tell me if you've seen my bag.'

'First things first,' was his maddening reply. 'One, you've just agreed to let me partner you this evening. Right?' Impatient at the delay, she nodded. 'Two, yes, I've seen your bag. I saw a hand take it.'

'But didn't you stop them?'

He was leaning back in his chair, legs crossed, arms folded, a smile softening the resolute line of his mouth. The music played, the dancers danced to its enticing rhythm.

'The hand I saw,' he stated softly, 'was mine. You want your bag?' He withdrew it from his pocket. 'You shall have it.'

Eagerly she seized it, then realised what he had done. 'Why did you hide it? You must have known I'd have a terrible fright!' She sank into her chair.

He leaned forward, hands clasped on the table. His brown eyes crinkled at the corners with amusement—or had they narrowed with cynicism? With his beard covering so much of his facial area, Lisa found herself struggling to identify his reactions.

'Either you're a consummate actress,' he remarked, 'or the momentary amnesia was purely Freudian.'

'What are you talking about?' she asked, indignation tightening her mouth. His only answer was a small smile. 'You don't mean I wanted an excuse to come back to you and used my bag for that purpose?'

'I opt,' he tantalised, 'for the second explanation.'

Lisa pushed back her chair and stood up. He caught her arm, urging her down. 'You agreed to be my partner this evening, Lisa, remember?' She sat down again.

Her name spoken by him sounded strange—and seductive. The feeling she had when he touched her, the effect on her of his low-pitched voice, the sheer masculine attractiveness of him combined to warn her to be on her guard. At twenty-three, her knowledge of worldly things was not so small that she did not know what he was after.

All the same, it would have been deluding herself to have pretended that his company for the rest of her stay would be serving her own purpose, too. She acknowledged that he had referred only to 'this evening'. Maybe, she thought, after one evening with him, she would prefer to spend the rest of her holiday alone! The thought made her smile and she turned this into one of acceptance to avoid questions.

'This evening, Mr Cameron,' she acquiesced.

He was still leaning forward, hands linked. Smiling, he commented, 'On the grounds that even a few hours in my company would be preferable to spending a lonely evening on your own?'

Lisa nodded, flashing him a smile. He watched the smile without returning it. She found it a curious experience. The man intrigued her, she had to admit. There was so much about him that held a certain mystery—including his partly-hidden face.

'Can I get you something to eat?' he offered, as if remembering his role as host. 'No? A drink, then?'

'Nothing, thank you.'

'Won't you call me Zander? Could you manage that?' His brown eyes were laughing, no doubt about that this time.

Lisa's heart beat faster as she laughed back at him. 'I think I might be able to. Shall I try it? Zander,' she essayed.

'Fine. She speaks my language.' His eyes glinted now, making her wonder just what he was thinking, making her wish, too, that she knew more about him. There was the merest overtone of an accent in his speech. 'You're English?' she ventured.

'*English?* With a name like mine? Good heavens, woman, I'm Scottish!' He watched as doubt dulled her eyes. His hand stretched out to touch hers fleetingly. 'Don't look so concerned. I'm proud of my heritage, just as I'm sure you're proud of yours?'

Lisa nodded. 'But we're both British,' she pointed out.

'We are indeed. Now, come on, my lovely lassie,' he lapsed into a broad Scottish accent and Lisa laughed, 'and dance wi' me to the bonnie music.' He removed his jacket and draped it round the chair back, then came to stand beside her.

After such an invitation, she knew she could not refuse. Nor did she wish to. That momentary brush of his hand had made her want to feel his touch again. Picking up her bag, she glanced at him, catching a half-veiled look that turned her heart over.

It was the same look as he had sent her way earlier—calculating and essentially sensual. Her fingers tightened round her bag. A feeling of defeat swept her, and of letdown. First Don, now this man. All right, so she knew why he was befriending her, and it had nothing to do with friendship. But did they all have to run so true to form?

'I'm sorry,' she began, 'I don't want to dance.'

His arm went round her waist, tugging her from the table. 'Oh, but I do, Lisa, I do.' He saw her fidgeting with her bag. 'Here, I'll take that.' He pushed it down into the pocket of his jacket which hung round the chair back. 'It'll be safe there.'

It was good to be in his arms—too good, Lisa told herself. He did not close the gap between them, but his hand on her back spread wide, while his other hand entwined with hers. He smiled down at her, but she felt too unsure of him to return his smile.

'It's okay, Lisa,' he said softly, 'I'm on the level. Underneath all this vegetation, there's an honest, cleanliving guy.'

Lisa laughed up at him. 'You shoot a good line. Is it effective on all your other casual pick-ups?'

He laughed. 'Hinting that it's not effective on you?' Total seriousness overtook his features and his eyes went cold, indicating complete withdrawal to another place and time. It took him about two seconds to return to normal. It took Lisa longer to recover from the freezing shock that had hit her at the frightening glimpse into his inner being. He went on, his smile easy, 'Believe me, I don't make a habit of forming convenient, shortlived relationships with women.'

There was the faintest whistle from the sidelines, and Lisa's head turned a fraction after Zander's. One of his three companions gave the thumbs-up sign. 'Och, away wi' ye,' he called to them in his broadest Scottish accent.

Lisa smiled, first at them, then up at Zander. 'Why are they falling about laughing?' she asked. 'Haven't they heard you speak like that before?'

He looked down at her, half-smiling. 'There are very

few indeed who have, Lisa. You bring out something in me.'

Her head went to one side. 'Like what, for instance?'

'A desire to play the fool, anything to make you laugh.'

There was a meaning in his words, but it eluded her. Even if she had worked it out, she knew it would also have worried her. She wanted to ask, Why, why? All she said was, 'I love laughing. It makes me feel good.'

'Then I must play the fool more often, mustn't I?' He had spoken softly, and now his lips rested briefly on her hair. Lisa did not object, although she knew that convention required it of her. I liked it, she told her conscience defiantly, I like him—too much, her conscience answered back.

'Your friends,' he asked, 'are they on their honeymoon?'

'Yes and no. They were engaged when this holiday was booked. One day Myra and Phil decided to get married, just like that. Five weeks ago yesterday. They knew this holiday was coming, so they delayed their honeymoon until now.'

'Do you mind being the odd one out?'

She looked up at him, unaware of the sadness of her expression. 'What do you think?'

'I think you look like a lost lamb.'

She laughed. 'Not at the moment. Not when I'm——' She realised just what she had been about to say. 'Forget it.' She looked away, across the heads of the dancers.

The music stopped, but he did not let her go. 'Forget what?' He gazed into her uplifted eyes. 'Not when you're with me?' She stared back. 'Be a devil,' he whispered, 'admit I'm right.'

Her head held stiffly, she answered, 'You're good company.'

He laughed loudly. 'As evasive an answer as any I've heard from a woman who refuses to admit she likes a guy!'

'I like you—so far. But—but don't you think this is a bit ridiculous? I saw you first this afternoon. I know nothing about you. You know more about me. At least you know I'm here on holiday. I can only guess that you aren't.'

Lisa was unprepared for his deep frown as he asked, 'Who told you? Or did you make an inspired guess?'

'Was it inspired?' She smiled up at him as they resumed their dancing. His good humour had returned. 'I was right that you're here to work, not play?'

'Right. I'm here to work—and play. Why not, in this climate, this incredible scenery all around us?'

'What is your work? Do you mind my asking?'

'Constructional engineering. Building hotels, roads——'

Her eyes were bright. 'I know what it means. I work for a constructional engineering company. Have you heard of it—Thistle International?'

'I've heard,' was his reply. 'Who hasn't in the line I'm in? Are you London-based?'

'Central London. Are you?' There was an eagerness in her tone which she hoped he had not heard.

He smiled down at her. 'The world is my oyster.'

'Oh.' She looked away, schooling her features to hide her disappointment. 'The company has offices in North Oxfordshire, too.'

'Have you been there?' She shook her head. 'You prefer to work in London?'

Head on one side, she considered. 'It has its advantages. But on balance, I think I'd prefer to work in the countryside.'

There was a pause, and she found he had pulled her closer to him. The experience was pleasant—too pleasant, she thought again. Her whole body felt alive. There was a strange excitement swirling round it, her whole metabolism had speeded up.

It worried her to have to acknowledge that this stranger was the source of her exhilaration. After this evening, since he was there to work—and after the 'play' she would be denying him at the end of it—she might never see him again.

CHAPTER TWO

WHEN the dance ended, he took her hand and pulled her to the door. 'I'd like a change of scenery. You don't mind, do you?'

'I've got a distinct feeling,' Lisa retorted, 'that it wouldn't matter if I did. You'd take no notice of my objections.'

The idea seemed to amuse him. 'What makes you think that?'

They were at the lift now, waiting for its arrival. 'I don't know—there's something about you.' She looked at him thoughtfully. The lift came and they stepped in. 'I keep getting the feeling I've seen you somewhere.'

He pressed the button. 'You have? Did I ever have a secret assignation with you? Maybe you were one of the females scattered about my past?' He was smiling broadly. He put a hand to his cheek. 'That can't be right. I'd have remembered you, no doubt about that.'

'I know! In a magazine. No, it wasn't. Not a magazine, but something like it.' They stepped out of the lift. He took her hand and walked her. 'But that's not right, either. You've got a beard, and in that picture I was thinking of, the man didn't have one.'

'I'd give it up, if I were you.' He was walking so fast she had to run beside him. They were going along the side of the roof restaurant. Inside, the lights were low and it seemed full of people. They came in the semi-darkness to a covered balcony.

The wind almost took Lisa's breath away. Wishing she had brought a jacket, she shivered, but Zander did not see it. He was gazing outward, yet his thoughts did not seem to be on the darkening hills of ash and lava which formed themselves into a saw-tooth pattern into the far distance.

The sounds from the restaurant broke the silence which seemed to Lisa to be inordinately long. Below,

21

civilisation brought its own raucous sounds which were
blatantly at odds with the stark silence of the far
reaches of the volcanic hills a mere lifting of the eyes
away.

'How much of the island have you seen?' Zander
asked at last.

'As far as I can see from this balcony in daylight. The
rest of the time we've spent down there on the beach.'

'Acquiring a suntan?' Unbelieving, he gazed at her.
'Is that what you came here for, just to lie on the
beach?'

'I'm one of three,' Lisa responded. 'If I find myself in
the minority, I have to go along with the others, don't
I? I doubt if they see much beyond each other at the
moment, anyway. And,' she felt she should defend her
friends, 'in the circumstances, it was good of them to let
me tag along.'

'Do you like "tagging along"?'

'I——' She felt the need to tell him the truth. 'No, I
don't. But it's not much fun going places with a crowd
of people you don't know, however friendly they are.'

For a few moments he did not respond, then he
turned and rested sideways against the balcony wall. He
smiled. 'You're not having much of a holiday, are you?
Knowing you'd be one too many, why didn't you cancel
your booking?'

'I offered, but they insisted that I came. They said
that after five weeks of marriage, they'd be like an old
married couple, but they still can't take their eyes off
each other.'

Smiling up at him, she saw his head was back with
laughter. 'Surprised as you sound?' he asked. 'If so, you
surprise me, having so recently had a man of your own.'

Her cheeks turned as pink as the sunset afterglow.
'He was a man, maybe mine for a little while, but
lover—no. And you can look as unconvinced as you
like, I'm speaking the truth.'

He reached out and pushed aside her wind-tossed
hair. The strands returned immediately and she smiled
up at him through them. His hands came out again and,
using both, he smoothed them back, creating a pathway

to her face. With palms cupping her cheeks, he turned her face a little and lowered his mouth to hers.

It was, Lisa thought, her eyes closed, a 'you're here, I'm here, too' kind of kiss. It contained no demand, no assessment of his chances later on of improving their acquaintance. For this reason, she enjoyed it, smiling up at him as the wind caught at them, billowing her skirt and running through his hair.

'Ye're a bonnie wee thing,' he declared softly, speaking again with a Scottish accent.

Lisa laughed into his eyes. 'How many women have you called that in your journeys abroad?' she asked, partly joking, yet badly wanting to know. It was dangerous, she warned herself, to like this keen-eyed, attractive stranger too much, and entirely stupid to enjoy a single kiss from him as much as she had.

The question had not pleased him, she could perceive that from the curious way his eyes dipped in temperature. Yet his smile returned swiftly as he answered, 'Hundreds, if not thousands. My women are scattered round the globe.'

He must have felt the stiffening of her body, since he pulled her closer, spreading his hand over the bare skin of her back where the sundress did not cover it. She shivered at his touch, yet he thought it was the wind and slipped his other arm around her waist.

'I was joking,' he told her, strangely intent. She nodded, staring into his eyes, discovering how they caught the lights behind them. 'It's not my habit to go around the world picking up women, taking what I want from them, then going on my way.'

Lisa searched his eyes, feeling a swirl of desolation curl itself round her like one of those cold gusts of wind. 'But you're going to make me an exception to your rule?'

'Do you want me to?' He was completely serious.

'Surely you know the answer to that?'

'Your encouragement this evening has given me hope that your answer would be "yes" if I asked.'

Her jerk as she disentangled from him gave him no time to tighten his hold. 'I'm sorry if I've given you that

impression.' She stared into the darkness. To her
dismay, her voice sounded choked. 'I don't understand
why a woman can't show that she likes a man without
his immediately taking it as a signal that she's willing to
sleep with him.'

For a long time, he looked at her. 'So you like me,'
he said. 'Well, that's a start.' His arm went across her
shoulders and her bare skin was electrified by his touch.
'Come on, I'll see you to your room.' He turned her and
she went with him.

'A start of what?' she demanded. They entered the lift.

'Of that friendship you seem to value so highly,' he
answered, smiling.

The noise of the dancers in the crowded room, the
sounds from the musicians which seemed to have
increased in volume contrasted starkly with the relative
peace of the darkness they had found outside.

'Come with me,' Zander commanded, holding Lisa's
hand. 'I'll get my jacket.'

On the way back to their table, they passed the three
men with whom Zander had dined. One had just
returned from the dance floor, his arm round the
shoulders of an attractive girl.

As they saw Zander, one of them raised a hand and
called, 'Hi, boss.' Lisa looked at him, then at the man
to whom the words had been addressed. She was
slightly behind Zander and noted that he did not even
turn his head in greeting.

Reaching their table, she said, 'One of your friends
called out to you.'

Zander was removing her bag from his pocket and
holding it out. 'Did he?' was the uninterested reply. He
shrugged into his jacket.

He led her to the door by a different route. 'Why,'
she asked, hurrying to keep up with him, 'did he call
you boss?'

In the lift, Zander's head was back, staring at the
advertisements on the lift's walls. 'Someone has to be in
charge of operations at a construction site on this scale.'
His eyes were moving as if he understood every word
the colourful advertisements held.

'You mean you're in charge?' she queried, her voice taking on a note of awe.

'My safety helmet doesn't exactly carry the word "boss" painted on it,' he stated dryly, 'but it's generally acknowledged that that is what I am.'

Lisa smiled at her handbag.

'What's the joke?'

'Only that top-class man needs top-class female companionship. Which means,' her eyes lifted boldly, 'I'm expendable after this evening. You'll quietly drop me and look for a female somewhat higher up the scale than a mere secretary.' They were out of the lift now. She gazed around. 'But you may be out of luck. There aren't that number of women administrators around, not even in these enlightened days.' Turning the key, she pushed open her door.

As she put a foot inside and switched on the light, he caught her shoulder, looked up and down the corridor and eased her in in front of him. The door swung closed, and he turned her to face him.

'Don't use sarcasm to try to score points off me, especially when the subject you're being so clever about is way out of your experience.' His brown eyes flared, then scorched a trail over the shape of her. 'Top-class male seeks out not his equal but his inferior where the away-from-home games of love are concerned. So,' his gaze narrowed on to her lips, 'come here, *inferior*, and let me get the real taste of you.'

Lisa tried to twist away, but his arms wrapped around her. He let her feel his increasing need and she cried, 'Don't! I'm not like that.'

His mouth prevented all further protest, the power in his lips fighting the determined stiffness of hers. In the end he won, forcing back her head and savouring her mouth's sweetness until she gasped for mercy.

Lifting his head, she saw that there was anger in his eyes and felt bewildered. She was the one he had plundered, so wasn't it she who should be furious?

Her pulses were pounding, not with anger but with excitement at his action, and the answering fire he had kindled inside her. Her mind told her that her arms which had crept round his neck were still there. Quickly, she removed them and looked for her bag, only to find that it had slipped to the floor.

His arms were still around her waist and when she looked back at him, she discovered his good, if cynical, humour had returned. 'Top-class man has indeed found himself a top-class woman,' he declared softly, 'one, moreover, who appears to have no *administrative* ambitions. Well, Lisa,' he lifted her chin, 'what's the answer—yes or no?'

Without even thinking, she ran a finger over his moustache, moving it down to his beard. 'Why all this?' she asked, without meeting his eyes. All the same, she saw his mouth harden, softening almost at once into a smile.

'Why not?' he answered reasonably.

'Why not?' she echoed, adding, 'To answer your other question it's "no". I'm sorry.'

He released her and walked away. To her chagrin, as he strode along the corridor, he did not once look back.

Lisa sat alone at the table. Her plate was scattered with the crumbs of the Continental breakfast she had just eaten. The coffee pot stood empty on the tray. Long ago she had given up looking for her friends, guessing they had eaten theirs in their room.

Her eyes had kept up their watch far longer for a sight of the tall, tanned figure of the man she had found herself thinking about with increasing frequency. Her thoughts just would not listen to her common sense. After her rejection of him last night, she told herself firmly that she would probably never see him again.

Her glance passed one more time over the line of people helping themselves to food from the long, white-covered tables set to one side of the large dining-room, then she wandered out to the short corridor leading to the main entrance foyer of the hotel.

Her friends were descending the curving staircase, hand in hand. They hurried to her, full of apologies which Lisa dismissed with a wide smile that did not come from her heart. All right, her less indulgent self fretted, so they're on a delayed honeymoon. But they know I'm here alone. Couldn't they make the effort to keep me company as they did when we first arrived?

'No escort?' Phil asked, looking past her. 'We thought we were doing you a kindness by letting you have him all to yourself for a while.'

Myra saw Lisa's frown. 'You know,' she added, a little anxiously, 'let you make your plans for the day.'

Lisa tried to ignore the skip of her heart. 'If you two want to go off on your own,' she suggested, 'don't worry about me. I'll be perfectly happy by the pool again.'

'That was exactly what we were going to do, anyway,' Myra exclaimed, and Lisa did not miss the relief in her voice.

Lisa had not really wanted to spend yet another day of their precious holiday sunbathing. The strange and mysterious landscape of which she had had mere glimpses beckoned irresistibly, but she had meant every word of what she had said to Zander Cameron about feeling lonely among a crowd of unfamiliar tourists.

'I'll go and change into my swimming things,' she told Myra, 'then I'll join you in our usual spot.'

On her way up the stairs, she passed two men whose faces were vaguely familiar. They were dressed in white overalls and each carried a safety helmet. Seeing this, she remembered the men's identity. They were two of Zander's three colleagues.

As they levelled with her on the wide staircase, one of the men, fair-haired and young, winked at her. Lisa started, surprised at the man's recognition. Something inside her resented just a little that meaningful wink, but she smiled back at him and he gave the thumbs-up sign. The meaning of this, if one had been intended, escaped her entirely.

Finding her friends' belongings near to the lava rocks which jutted from the sea, forming a small reef on the golden sand, Lisa dropped down, placing her bag of clothes and towels beside her. It was not difficult identifying Myra in her scarlet two-piece, and Phil was not far away from his wife.

Myra saw her and beckoned and Lisa waved back. The sea looked invitingly blue. The sun was hot and here, in this sheltered bay, its warmth was not cooled by the constant breeze.

Her friends shouted greetings as she waded in deeply enough to dip herself and swim. After a while, she stood up and looked about her, only to find that Myra and Phil had returned to the beach. For a few moments, she watched them as they struggled playfully with each other, then she stared at the scattering of yachts which the hotel guests had hired. Other people were windsurfing, skimming over the sea at the whim of the strong wind which blew constantly.

Deciding to give her companions a little more time together, Lisa turned on to her back and floated, letting her eyes drink in the intense blueness of the sky. Here and there a palm tree grew high enough to drift into her line of vision. Treading water, she studied the contrast between the rough brown of the lava rocks with the bright green of the shrubs which had been cultivated to climb the slope of the beach towards the hotel building.

She had, she decided, given her friends long enough to recover from the excitement of their swim. As she waded out, the sand felt warm to her feet. She reached for a towel and smiled down at them as they lay contentedly in each other's arms. Lucky you, she thought, to have found each other. There was, she denied vehemently to herself, no envy of them in her heart. Was there?

It was mid-afternoon now and Lisa found herself lying once more beside her friends' prone figures. She had watched with a feeling of envy the coach-load of hotel guests as they had driven away towards the hills.

Involuntarily, her eyes had searched all around her for a glimpse of Zander Cameron, but she knew she would not find him. What man as attractive as he was would bother again with a girl who had turned him away as decisively as she had done from her bedroom door last night?

Even now, as Phil slowly and lovingly massaged

suntan oil on to his wife's back, Lisa's gaze wandered hopefully, yet without real hope, from one group to another, knowing that even if she found him, he could well be laughing and lying with another woman.

Myra and Phil, entangled as usual, seemed to be sleeping. Lisa rose quietly and tied back her hair, still damp from her recent swim. She was making for the reef of lava rocks. As she clambered on to them, they felt rough to her feet and hands and she wondered at her wisdom in venturing on to their warm, abrasive angles and slopes.

Finding a reasonably comfortable place to sit, she dangled her feet in a frothing pool, delighting in the water's coolness yet loving the heat of the sun on her back. Someone shouted and her head turned automatically. A man stood nearby on the sands. He was fair-haired and wore a white sun-shirt and trunks. His feet were bare and he had a knowing look on his smiling face.

Calming her heartbeats, Lisa recognised the man and smiled, turning back to watch the clear water. For some reason she could not explain, she did not like him, despite the fact that he had never actually spoken to her. If I ignore him, she reasoned, he'll go away. There must have been a fault in her reasoning, since she heard the crunch and slide of footsteps approaching from behind her.

'All alone?' The man lowered himself to sit nearby.

Lisa restrained herself from making the obvious retort and stayed silent.

'Enjoying your holiday?'

Lisa nodded, conceding that the man had perseverance, but what man hadn't, she thought wryly, when in pursuit of a female?

'Lucky you,' the man persisted. 'I'm here to work.'

Lisa knew she would have to give some kind of response. Looking the man over, she commented, 'It doesn't look like it.'

The man grinned, pleased to have coaxed some words out of her. 'We all need time off for fun, don't we?' Receiving no answer, he persisted, 'You don't look as though you're having much fun.' He touched her arm fleetingly. 'We could have fun together?'

He was doing his best, Lisa thought, smiling to herself. He was toeing the moral line to test her, ready at the slightest encouragement to step over it should she give the smallest signal. Carefully, she slipped down into the shallow pool and stepped across the barrier of rocks into the main bay.

'Hey,' the man called, 'don't walk out on me, just as we're getting to know each other!'

She watched the swirls and eddies her moving feet made as she waded to the beach. 'Thanks for talking to me,' she called over her shoulder, 'but I'm quite happy on my own, or with my friends.' He had caught up with her now. 'I'm not looking for a casual holiday relationship.' She smiled at him. 'Sorry.'

Searching for her companions, she saw that they had gone, obviously thinking again that they were being tactful.

'Ah, well,' the man affected a sigh, 'can't win 'em all.' With a lift of his hand, he went on his way.

Lisa picked up a towel and bent to dry her legs and feet. Her head was drawn round involuntarily and she saw the man in white give a thumbs-down signal to a taller, leaner man, whose body was deeply tanned and whose beard and longer than average hair covered much of his face.

They were looking at her and talking. Zander Cameron was nodding as the other man spoke. Lisa felt a rush of fury catch at her lungs. So he had been testing her, using one of his colleagues as bait!

Turning her back on them, she pulled at the ribbon and rubbed at her hair with more vigour than was really necessary to dry it. Two hands rested on hers, stilling them and imprisoning them on top of her head. Standing stiffly and scarcely breathing, she compressed her lips. He had had the audacity to come down to continue their relationship from where it had stopped last night!

Without warning, she twisted away and stared at him stormily. 'Now you've tested me by remote control and found me morally upstanding, you've condescended to give me the benefit of your company again!' She lowered the towel and her hair descended fluffily about her shoulders. 'Well, I don't want it, thanks. You can go and bestow it on another woman. There are plenty for you to choose from.'

His eyes seemed for a few seconds to take up the coolness of the ever present wind, then he turned on his heel and made his way up the slope of the beach. His back was straight, his tanned body lean and tough. His shorts were fawn, showing the dark hair on his browned and muscled legs.

He was walking away and, she had to face it, he was walking out of her life. The moment she became appalled at the thought that she had lost him through her foolish pride, it came to her forcibly that she had been equally foolish in allowing him to become, in such a short space of time, so important to her happiness.

'Zander, don't go ...' The plea was uttered spontaneously and she cursed herself for revealing to him her vulnerability. She had put a weapon into his hands and, being the man he was, she was sure he would use it.

He had stopped dead in his tracks but did not turn. Holding her breath, Lisa waited for him to continue. Instead, he walked in a semi-circle, his footsteps making imprints in the sand. Facing her, but at a slight distance, he asked,

'Why? I'm useful, is that it? As an escort, maybe, as a male to make up a foursome—or did you have it in mind that you and I should be a cosy twosome after all?'

His distant manner, the sarcastic attack on her motives deprived her momentarily of an answer. He was lifting the weapon she had handed him. A few more moments, and he would bring it down and her with it.

'I like you, Zander—I did tell you. I like your friendship, too.' It's more than friendship you feel for him, her heart was saying, much more. How stupid can I get, she reproached herself, to let myself become entangled again so quickly? Didn't I learn anything about the unreliability of men from the way Don behaved?

This man was different from Don in every way, she thought with a warming confidence. You only had to stand near him to feel the waves of strength coming from him, like rock that gave out the heat of that day's sun for a long time after the sun had set.

He was coming towards her and she could feel it now, that veiled power. It was wrapping about her, without even so much as a touch of his finger. He smiled down at her and her tremulous greeting gave away her pleasure at his banishment of the barrier between them.

His arms came open and she went into them, her cheek resting against his chest. As his beard brushed her forehead, she pushed it aside and laughed up at him. 'It gets in the way,' she commented. 'Why don't you shave it off?'

He stared at the sea, then his gaze returned to her. 'That I will not do.'

'But I want to see the man beneath it.'

His smile caressed her face. 'Maybe you wouldn't like that man.'

'Maybe I would *love* that man.'

A lightning flash of remoteness zigzagged across his face, then it was gone. 'That you would not do, my bonnie lassie.' She smiled as his face came close and he gnashed his teeth near her mouth. 'You would *hate* him.'

His lips softened and came briefly to rest on hers. When he lifted his head, he remarked, 'I had to catch that smile of yours. I'll wrap it securely round my heart.'

'And keep it there for ever?'

'For ever.'

Lisa smiled, but felt strangely troubled. 'You'll never throw it away, not even when my holiday's over and we never see each other again?' He continued to gaze into her eyes. 'Even,' she persisted, 'when you've got a wife and family?' She stared into the bush of his beard as if it were an impenetable forest and she could not fight her way through to the daylight. She was in a mental maze, searching for a future that was not there.

'I told you, I wander the world. What would a man like me do with a wife and kids?'

It was a question to which she could not possibly provide the answer. Her eyes closed to hide the quick pain she had felt. His hold had loosened a little and she saw her friends standing at the top of the steps watching them.

It seemed they were about to show tact again and withdraw, so Lisa lifted her arm full-length to wave. 'My friends,' she explained, 'they're up there——'

'Let them alone. They only want each other. They're probably delighted you've found yourself a partner.'

His voice sounded so gruff she looked up at him. He was staring out to sea again, then, without looking at her, his hands started kneading at the tight flesh around her bare waist. It was as though his thoughts were causing him pain and that he needed her—or any woman, she reminded herself sharply—in order to ease that pain.

When Lisa glanced behind him again, she discovered that her friends had gone. She had to admit she was glad this time that they had acted with such discretion.

His hands strayed to her scantily-covered hips, rubbing them as if attempting to massage away a newly-inflicted hurt. Not to me, she realised intuitively, but to himself.

It seemed that he at last became aware of his actions. The agitated movements ceased, his palms rested on her hips and he held her puzzled eyes. She had loved the stroking feel of his touch, unconscious though it had been, yet she could not understand why an urge to reach up and comfort him had swept through her.

'Zander?' The colour of his eyes seemed to lighten. 'Who were you touching just now? It wasn't me, it couldn't have been. You were so far away. Some girl you know?'

He smiled faintly. 'Some girl I know.'

Lisa nodded, hoping the action would tell him that she understood his intention had not been to arouse her but had been caused by thoughts of someone he missed badly while he was so far away from her.

Crouching down beside her belongings, she scrabbled in her beach bag for a comb. He dropped beside her, stretching his long legs and resting back on his elbows. Lisa tugged at the tangles and tied back her hair, sitting beside him.

Without turning her head, Lisa asked, 'Taking time off?'

A finger ran slowly down her spine from her yellow bra top to her minute swimming briefs, making her straighten, then turn, smiling.

'I'm the boss,' he stated, 'I don't have to ask permission.'

Lisa drew pictures in the golden sand. 'It must be nice to be able to say, Right, men, peasants or scum, or whatever bosses call their subordinates——'

A muscle-powered arm hooked itself around her neck and pulled her backwards and against its owner. 'You've got the impudence of the devil, Miss Maynard. What the hell do you think I call the men who work *with* me?'

Desperate fingers plucked at his arm. 'Bill, Johnny, Jack—how do I know? And please let me go.'

He ran his other hand over the front of her, skimming her breasts and coming to rest on her waist. 'You're an armful of sheer delight,' he mused, and her head tipped back against his chest to look upside down at him. His eyes were half-closed and she caught that narrow, contemplating look again that made her heart leap and join her already speeding pulses in a race-to-the-finish.

'How do you know?' she asked, then realised the challenge she had thrown down.

Protesting as he rolled her over and into his arms, she lay breathless beside him. The throb of his heart filled her ear and her hand rested on the ridges of his rib-cage beneath his taut flesh. His hand covered hers and they lay quietly, hearing the small waves break on the shore, other people's voices come and go on the wind.

'I'm thirsty,' Lisa announced, only to be taken by surprise as he half-rose, turned her face and kissed her.

'Is that better?' he asked, and as she shook her head mutely, staring into his eyes, he repeated the kiss, penetrating her lips this time, then repeating the question.

'Yes, yes,' she answered firmly, struggling free, 'and I didn't mean that, you know I didn't.'

He rested on his elbow and smiled lazily back. As she raked in her bag, she looked up at him. 'Isn't your beard a nuisance in this heat?'

'That's my business, isn't it?' There was an edge, no doubt about it, and Lisa frowned. Seeing her uncertainty, he went on more gently, 'I told you, you wouldn't like the man underneath this bushiness.'

Drawing out a large bottle of mineral water, she retorted, 'That's pure nonsense. You're the same man with or without it.'

'I thought you were thirsty.'

Lisa smiled, unfastening the screw-top. 'Change of subject agreed.' In the act of lifting the bottle to her mouth, she paused. 'I haven't brought a cup. Do you object if I look unladylike for a few minutes?'

He rolled on to his side, head propped on hand. 'Know something? I'd love you to be unladylike for much longer than a few minutes. Preferably when it's dark and there's a full moon and there's no one about.'

Her only reply was to give a quick smile and take a drink from the mouth of the upraised bottle. As she lowered it, she felt the mineral water running down her chin. Busy with searching for a paper tissue, she did not see a large, tanned hand come out. With the back of it, Zander wiped the dampness away, drying his own hand on his shorts.

'Thanks,' she said. 'I would have done that myself, except that I didn't want to offend the susceptibilities of the meticulous man underneath your beard.'

'Cheeky imp!' He was on his knees and holding her throat with his hand. His head lowered, then he stopped and their eyes locked as a very different feeling began to form.

Seconds went by, breath-depriving, nerve-tightening. Lisa's lips throbbed in anticipation of receiving his.

They did not come. The moment had passed. He returned to his earlier position and, after a moment, she offered him the bottle. He took it, gulping a few mouthfuls, then wiping his own mouth with his hand.

Lisa replaced the top and returned it to the beach-bag. Staring out to sea, she sat with her knees bent, her hands clasped round them. It was taking her over, the pleasure she experienced in being with this man. She hardly knew him, yet she felt she had known him for years, so much did she feel at one with him. It was impossible to judge his feeling about her. In any case, she knew it was foolish to believe he felt anything for her except as one more female in his long list of conquests.

Curious as to where his thoughts might be, she glanced at him over her shoulder. He smiled back. For him, it seemed, the flare of feeling between them had died down, yet she could still feel the scorch marks in the environs of her heart.

CHAPTER THREE

Lisa stood in her room staring past the billowing curtains and through the opened glass doors which led to the balcony. The sea was darkening slightly as if in anticipation of the approach of night.

Her thoughts were on her parting with Zander. Dine with me, he had said, and it had not been a question. I'm dining with Myra and Phil, she had replied, but he had told her briskly, Tonight you're not.

Even if he had not been so assertive about it, she would not have wanted to argue. It would be the afternoon's pleasure extended. When her other self tried to warn, Remember Don. Keep this man at a distance, preferably on the other side of the world, she told the tiny voice to let her be. A holiday friendship, that's all it is, she'd told it. If I lose my heart, it's *my* heart, isn't it?

Picking up the telephone, she dialled Myra and Phil's extension. Myra answered and when she heard about the dinner arrangements, she was delighted.

'He's fallen for you, Lisa. We watched you for a couple of minutes this afternoon and I can tell, dear. Trust Aunty Myra to recognise love at first sight when she sees it!'

Lisa had denied every word, but Myra wished her luck. 'Make the most of it,' she advised before ringing off. 'If you like him, and I think you do, let your hair down. After all, when the holiday's over, you'll never meet him again, will you?'

It was with this thought in mind that she stared at her wristwatch, counting the seconds as the hands moved to the exact moment of their prearranged meeting. She was trying so hard not to seem too eager, yet her feet were clamouring to be on their way to the lift. Why was she delaying, just for the sake of appearances?

There was so little time until the final day, the

moment of parting, so little time to be in his company . . . In a moment, she was locking her bedroom door behind her and making for the lift. As she stepped out of it, he was there waiting, leaning against the wall and staring at nothing. Looking round idly as if resigned to a long wait, he saw her. Never, she thought, would she forget the lighting up of his eyes, nor the shining smile which illuminated his features as she went towards him.

Refusing to ask herself, What does it mean? she put out her right hand in a spontaneously formal gesture. He took it in his left and pulled her towards him.

Tipping back her head, she asked, 'Am I going to be the odd one out at your usual table for four, instead of my own table for three?'

'That's right,' he flicked back, 'but you'll have to sit on my knee. Do you mind?'

Laughing up at him, she swung his hand in her happiness. A quick look around told her that Myra and Phil had not yet appeared for dinner. 'Where are your colleagues?' she asked.

'Back there at the bar.' He guided her to a table in the shadows, following the head waiter who pulled out her chair with a flourish. She nodded her thanks when he handed her the menu.

'Is the bar where you would be,' she questioned, 'if you hadn't picked me out as your holiday woman?' She was deliberately provoking him, but she did not care. Waiting for a swift answer to her touch of impudence, she was surprised by his response.

'That's where I would have been if you hadn't picked me out with your wide blue eyes and your "little girl lost" look.'

'*I* picked you out? I saw you looking at me with a—with a look I didn't like.'

Zander laughed at her indignation. 'You loved it, be honest. It pleased the femininity in you knowing that a man desired you. Especially as you'd just split with your boy-friend. That in itself is a traumatic event.'

'Oh? In what way?' She peered at him over the menu.

He looked back at her over his. 'The breaking up of any close relationship is alleged to be shattering.'

Lisa studied her menu again without really reading it. 'I heard that, too. I wouldn't know, but maybe you've had first-hand experience?'

There was a long pause, during which Lisa did not dare look at him. Her question had bordered on indelicacy and she did not know him well enough to be able to judge his response.

He said at last and she stole a look at him, seeing his unexpectedly serious expression, 'I suggest that, for the remainder of our acquaintance, we take each other at face value.'

'No past, no future, only present?' At his nod, she continued, 'I don't mind, I don't mind at all.' I do, I do, she thought, hiding her taut lips with the menu.

'Right.' His voice was businesslike, surprisingly so. 'Let's make our decisions about what we're going to eat.'

Lisa tried to understand the Spanish words, found the translations underneath strangely blurred and put aside the menu. 'You choose, Zander. You must know the taste of all those dishes on offer back to front by now.'

The waiter came discreetly at Zander's call, and wrote quickly on his notepad. Lisa's eyes wandered and she saw her friends. They noticed her at the same moment and waved, Myra smiling her encouragement. Zander watched the byplay detachedly, but with a smile. A moment later they were doing their best to pretend she wasn't there.

'They look pleased to have you off their backs.'

The touch of something cold made Lisa shiver inside. 'Is that why you're spending your time with me? To let the honeymooners get away from their nuisance of a third party, surplus to their requirements?'

The wine which Zander had ordered was brought to stand beside the table. He asked, his eyes following the draped neckline of her burnt orange-coloured dress, 'Is that why you think I'm befriending you?'

'Befriending?' The question should have stayed in her mind. By speaking it aloud, she had revealed to him her dislike of it.

'Friendship. Isn't that the thing you value so much between a man and a woman?'

Other men and other women, maybe, she thought, but not you. 'I think you're befriending me because——' Then she recalled his welcome as she had stepped out of the lift, but she had to continue now she had started. 'Because you're bored with the company of your colleagues and——' He was waiting, eyebrows raised just a little dauntingly. 'And you felt in need of a woman's company.'

For just a moment his eyes hardened, then they softened, but his words were a torment. 'Clever of you to guess, Lisa. I'll return your doubtful compliment. I think you're allowing me to latch on to you to fill the void, no matter how temporarily, that the loss of your boy-friend left.'

He had spoken in a now-beat-that voice, but she did not even try. Instead, she said, 'Didn't we agree—no past, no future?'

'Dodgy wee thing, aren't you?' he commented, leaning back as their appetisers were placed in front of them. 'First you pack a punch with an impudent challenge, then you duck when my return punch comes your way and offer me your hand calling a truce.'

Lisa, tackling the food with relish, smiled across the table. 'I'm a clever wee lassie, aren't I?' she asked with a commendable imitation of a Scottish accent.

He laughed loudly, pausing in the act of raising a forkful of food to his mouth. 'I'll have to coach you to help you improve your Scottish accent.' He continued eating.

'Coaching's not necessary. After a few weeks with you around me speaking your lilting Scottish phrases, I'll be able to speak it perfectly myself.' Her smile was knocked clean cold as she replayed what she had just said. Putting down her fork, she said, 'Please forget that statement.'

His features recovered from their loss of warmth. 'My memory facility has obediently stopped functioning. No yesterday, no tomorrow.' He lifted the glass which had been filled for him. 'Let's drink to this time, this place, this moment.'

Lisa lifted her glass, touched his and they drank.

Over coffee, Zander asked, 'Would you like a tame, if inexperienced personal courier to take you around the island?'

Her eyes shone. 'You mean you would take me?'

'Turn up the brightness control of those lovely eyes of yours every time you look at me and I'll do anything for you, my lassie.'

'Zander,' her hand reached out to cover his as it lay on the table, 'if you show me the island's interior, I'll love you for ever.'

'You will?' He smiled, making as if to leave. 'Let's go. The offer of a lifetime in your arms is too wonderful to resist!'

Lisa laughed. 'You know I didn't mean this minute, don't you?'

He studied her curved lips. His shoulders, whose breadth was emphasised by the cut of his lightweight jacket, lifted and fell. 'So I'll have to wait until tomorrow for the lifetime to start.'

Her attention was caught by the patch of dark chest hair which the open neck of his blue shirt revealed. 'Lifetimes,' she declared, looking at him at last, 'are out.'

A flicker shot across his eyes, then they were back to normal. 'Lifetimes are out,' he repeated, tossing the remaining contents of his glass down his throat.

As they left the restaurant, Lisa turned to wave to Myra and Phil. They had gone, but Lisa caught the eye of one of Zander's three colleagues. It was the fair-haired man, and once again he gave the "thumbs-up" sign. Turning away irritably, she found that Zander had been watching, too.

'I wish that friend of yours wouldn't keep doing that. There must be a reason. Is he cheering you on? Have you got a bet with him that you'll get me into bed with you before my holiday's over?'

They were in the foyer now and Zander was smiling as he walked beside her. 'No, but you've given me an idea.'

Lisa tugged her hand free of his and made for the

stairs, but she did not get far. His arm swung round her waist, compelling her to a stop.

'Canna ye tak' a wee joke?' he asked, his eyes bright, his Scottish accent emphasised.

Lisa's anger evaporated at once and she laughed up at him. Held close against his body, she was conscious of its every angle. His arms were still around her waist and her own lifted slowly to encircle his. As the surrounding voices faded in, she became embarrassed and disengaged from him quickly.

'What are you doing this evening?' she asked. 'Going dancing again?'

'If that's what you want.'

'Don't worry about me. I only agreed to have dinner with you. If you want to dance, there are plenty of girls back there who'd be delighted to have you as their partner. You know, girls who've come together here but are lonesome just the same.'

'This lonely girl,' his hand rested on her shoulder, 'is all I need.'

'Sorry,' she swung to the stairs, 'but "this girl's" not for "needing". I'm going up to my room.'

He was striding up the stairs beside her, saying nothing, giving her no indication of his intention. At the top of the second staircase, Lisa was a little breathless with the speed of the climb—she had done her utmost to keep up with his deliberately fast pace—and with agitation as to what her next move should be.

They paused and she turned to him. 'Thank you for seeing me this far. Thanks, also, for your company over the meal.'

He grinned, plainly guessing her strategy. 'That's okay. I enjoyed myself.'

As she walked along to her door, she raked in her bag for her key, trying to pretend he was not still beside her. 'Let me,' he said, extracting the key from her fingers and opening the door.

With irritation, she took back the key. Turning before she went in, she wished him goodnight. She had managed to convey her resolve through the timbre of her voice, but she hid from him the lack of it in her eyes by taking her time in putting down her room key.

When she turned back to close the door, she found that he had closed it for her. He was still there, leaning against it, hands in pockets, watching her.

'Do you want me to go?' he asked.

Looking in the mirror past herself at his reflection, she answered slowly, 'You can stay a while, as long——' she picked up a perfume bottle, put it down, 'as long as you don't regard it as an invitation to stay, a—a signal, as you'd call it, telling you I'm ready and willing and——'

'I won't.' Zander lifted himself from the door and trod the carpet to the opened doors to the balcony. There he stared out until she joined him, when he moved to allow her to pass on to the balcony. He had not touched her, yet she was so attuned to him now, it was almost as if they had made physical contact.

Lisa sank on to the beach chair, first brushing it free of sand which had blown upward from the bay. Stealing a glance, she saw that he was still staring out and wondered if he was really seeing the deepening blue of the sea as darkness approached.

He became aware of her as if feeling her eyes on him and his slow smile turned him back into the man she had come to know. Not only to know, she thought, staring at the sea herself as he occupied the other chair, but for whom, she discovered to her dismay, she had begun to feel a deep affection.

Not only a deep affection, her thoughts snaked relentlessly on, but a need, an aching need for the feel of him against her. It was a holiday acquaintance, she reminded herself firmly, no more, no less. It was certainly not a holiday romance—a kiss, joking, laughter, what could they be called but a pleasing acquaintance?

'Lisa?' His voice caressing her name dragged her from her thoughts. 'Your friends are down there.'

Leaning closer to the balcony rail, she watched her friends clambering over the lava rocks on which she had sat and dabbled her feet earlier in the sun's heat.

'They're like a couple of kids,' she commented.

'I caught a trace of envy.'

Her head swivelled as she started to deny his statement, but she shrugged instead. 'They've found happiness together, and I'm glad. I can only hope it lasts.'

'Which it didn't with you?'

'If you're referring to my ex-boy-friend, we never shared that kind of feeling.'

'Is that why he found another girl, one maybe who was high-spirited and outgoing?'

'Unlike me, I suppose you're implying?' Her fiery eyes rested on him. 'I can laugh and be foolish with the best of them.'

'I'm sure you can.' His tone was both soothing and kindling.

'You know I can.' It annoyed her that he seemed to be enjoying her anger. 'If you must know, the girl who took him away was bossy and overbearing. He seemed to love it.'

'Some men do. I don't.'

Her head went back, enjoying the joke. 'Really? You could have fooled me.'

Zander leant back and crossed his legs, looking at her askance in the way that she recalled from the first time she saw him. 'I could,' he remarked, 'make you pay for that bit of sarcasm. But I won't——' his eyes wandered over her, 'yet.' A lightning-touch of excitement sped through her system at his look and his words.

There was a squeal from the beach and they watched as Myra almost overbalanced from a rock. Phil's arms caught her and held her fast. Lisa moved her eyes from their transparent delight in each other, overwhelmed by a frightening feeling of wanting to be loved in that way, too. On no account would she admit to herself by whom she wanted to be loved.

'Where do you live?' Zander asked.

'In the suburbs west of London, not too far from where I work.'

'Alone?'

It did not occur to her to remind him of their promise

not to probe into each other's lives. 'With Myra in a two-roomed flat, until she married Phil. Now I live there alone.' Her head swung round, her hair lifted by the movement. 'Where do you live, Zander?'

In the gathering darkness she wondered if she had imagined the hardening of his brown eyes. 'I told you, I wander the world.'

'But you must have a place you call your own, surely? A roof over your head.' He seemed in no hurry to reply. 'Or is it someone else's roof?'

His head turned slowly and she discerned a narrow look on his face. 'For a passing acquaintance, you're asking a lot of probing questions.' He jerked his chair to face her. 'It's my business, isn't it, Miss Maynard, on whose pillow I lay my weary head?'

Had he known how much his answer would hurt? 'You asked me questions like that. I didn't bite your head off. I answered them civilly.'

He rose lazily and stretched out a hand, taking one of hers and pulling her up. His fingers lifted her chin. 'Accept my apologies. Now do I merit a smile?' His brown eyes regarded her so comically, she obliged. He lowered his head and caught the smile with his lips. 'Another to add to my collection.'

'What will you do with them?' she asked, her smile widening. 'Put them in an album like a stamp collector?'

The sky was dark now and in the shadow thrown by the lights in the room, she could not see his eyes' expression. 'I fancy that,' he answered, 'almost as much as I fancy you.'

Ignoring his provocative statement, she persisted, 'Then, when we've parted for ever, you'll tear each one out of the album and replace them with even more precious smiles—from the woman you love enough to marry.'

His fingers pinched her chin, hurting her. 'Love is an emotion you and I do not discuss,' he stated roughly. He drew her backwards into the room, reaching out to close the doors. Then he kissed her, the pressure of the action pushing back her head until her arms gripped the sleeves of his jacket. His finger followed the draped neckline of her dress, finding an entrance and making contact with her skin. His hand was cool and subtly caressing, slipping upwards to her shoulder, resting there as if waiting for a shake in reprimand. It did not come, and the trailing fingers continued in their search, moving downwards slowly, so slowly it failed to penetrate Lisa's misty mind under the potent influence of Zander's kiss.

When he found and moulded the swelling shape, a gasp was caught in Lisa's throat. She struggled to lift her head and he let her. Staring into his intense brown eyes, she whispered, 'Zander?'

His only answer was to pull her against him and lower his head, impatient to reclaim her mouth. As his hand possessed and teased the hardening fullness, a sensation of delight filled all that was flowing and throbbing within her.

It did not matter that she knew nothing about him, that his identity was wrapped in a mystery she would never solve. She knew only that she had felt for no man, not even Don, what she was beginning to feel for this puzzling stranger. His touch excited, his whole personality drew around her a magic circle which, whenever he was there, excluded the whole world except themselves.

When he freed her mouth, his hand gave up its intimate hold, but he did not entirely release her. 'I find you irresistible,' he said, his voice husky.

'I don't know how you can say that,' she declared, 'when we only met yesterday.'

'I couldn't take my eyes off you from the first moment I saw you. How's that for attraction at first sight?'

Lisa frowned, musing, 'Only yesterday, yet it seems so much longer.' With an agitated movement, she pulled free, straightening her dress. 'We mustn't get—get involved with each other. I don't think we should meet again.'

His arms crossed over her back, pulling her close again. 'Why fight it? A few days out of time, that's all it will be. The attraction's there for both of us. Give in to it, Lisa.'

Her hands found his shoulders. 'I'm just getting over being walked out on. Don was nice, pleasant, but I know now he wasn't right for me. All the same, it hurt.' Her eyes lifted from contemplating his strong, brown neck. 'I don't want any more pain, Zander.'

He was serious now, so serious it startled her. 'Are you saying that it would give you pain to part from me, even after only two days of our knowing each other?'

Mutely, she gazed at him. If she told him, 'Yes', she would give away a secret which she had not yet told even herself. If she answered 'No', she would be lying. Which was why she stayed silent.

He did not fill that silence. He continued to gaze at her, but to Lisa's over-sensitive eyes, he seemed to have retreated into himself. He was going from her, she could feel it. Her fingers clung to his shoulders. Her cheek found his chest.

His hands moved, running up and down her hips, waist, breasts, as they had when they had stood together earlier on the beach. She felt his agitation and in a purely instinctive gesture placed her own hands over his and stilled them at her waist, in an inexplicable effort to offer him comfort.

Gently, he put her from him, brushing her disappointed mouth. 'Goodnight, Lisa.'

Watching him go to the door, she experienced a sweeping sense of deprivation. 'Will I—will I see you tomorrow?'

He smiled faintly. 'Look around. Maybe I'll be there.'

Lisa rose early, dressing in white slacks, apricot-coloured round-necked shirt and short-sleeved white jacket. Combing her deep-brown hair, she found grains of sand clinging to the comb. The wind had deposited them there, she guessed, as she had lain on the beach.

To her surprise, Myra and Phil were waiting in the hotel foyer. 'Hope we didn't do the wrong thing yesterday,' Myra said as, with Phil, they made for their table in the restaurant.

'You looked so cosy together,' Phil offered, 'we thought it would be a shame to break it up.'

Lisa smiled. 'That's okay.' She took her seat. 'To be honest, I was quite pleased you'd guessed right. We——' she corrected herself, 'I like him.' How did she know if he returned that liking? He'd said a lot of flattering things, but men did, didn't they, when they wanted a woman?

'Are you seeing him today?' Myra asked, brightly interested. 'I mean, there's only a limited time for you to get to know him, and——'

'You know what they say,' her husband prompted, 'holiday romances don't last.'

Lisa laughed, then sobered as she caught sight of the group of four men who had entered. Zander appeared yet again not to have seen her.

Looking down at her empty plate, she informed her companions, 'Yes, I am seeing him today. He's right over there, immersed in a mini-conference with his colleagues.'

'Colleagues?' Phil queried, surprised. 'You mean he's here to *work*?'

'That's right. Constructional engineering. What' more, they call him "boss". I've heard them.'

'Boss of what?' Myra asked. 'Where's he from?'

Lisa lifted her shoulders. 'I asked. He wouldn't tell me. Wanders the world, he said.'

'Maybe he's a contractor. You know, hires out his services as a consultant. That way, he would be abroad a lot.'

'Has he heard of our company, Thistle International?' Myra asked.

Lisa nodded, and decided to steer the conversation into safer waters. She did not, for some reason, want to keep talking about Zander Cameron. Her friendship with him was too precious a thing to be discussed so dispassionately by others, even if those others were her friends.

'I'm getting myself some breakfast. You two coming?'

To reach the long, self-service tables, it was necessary to pass near the four men. Their discussion absorbed them completely, Lisa noted disappointedly. Her plate filled, she walked once again within speaking distance, all set to be ignored for the second time. She was startled when the fair-haired man turned his head and winked at her.

The action did not go unobserved by the man they called 'boss'. Cold eyes, brown and contemplative, rested on her, his mouth unsmiling, his hair springing thick and dark. I might as well be a stranger, Lisa lamented, yet angry deep inside for the unpredictable and needling ways of the man.

Now he knows me, now he doesn't, she fretted. Two can play at that, she determined, taking her seat and laughing with her friends. When the four men rose and Zander Cameron left with them without a glance in her direction, her carefree manner dropped away. She would not have cared if Myra and Phil had noticed her failure to continue to enjoy their jokes, but her withdrawal into her own thoughts seemed to slip their notice entirely.

With her friends, she spent the morning patronising the hotel's shops. Then they wandered round the capital town of Arrecife, looking at the white-walled, flat-roofed buildings, gazing at the balconied apartment blocks and crossing the streets between cars and vans.

All the time the sun heated their skins, while the wind blew their hair and flapped at their clothes. They found their way to the white-walled church of San Gines, then gazed at the fishing vessels which formed, they had been told by a courier at the hotel, the largest fishing fleet in the Canary Islands.

Arriving back at the hotel, Myra and Phil raced up the hotel staircase, believing that Lisa was following. Turning, Myra discovered that she was still in the hotel foyer, waving to them to continue. 'See you for lunch,' Myra mouthed, and Lisa nodded.

Telling herself she needed a rest before going to her room, Lisa sank on to one of the red-upholstered chairs in the hotel foyer. Deep down, she admitted to herself the real reason. Her eyes were in on the secret and searched the foyer for a tall, bearded figure. At her eyes' first radar-sweep of the carpeted area, they failed to pick out their target. Then they found it and homed in.

He was leaning against the bar, glass in hand, in that familiar and maddeningly indolent way, adding up her feminine attributes as if he had never seen her before. His glass touched his lips, yet his eyes continued to observe her. He was near enough, she calculated angrily, to see the surge of colour that dyed her cheeks.

This, she thought, clutching her bag, is my chance to pretend he doesn't exist. Deliberately returning his stare, she swept towards the stairs, her back straight, her footsteps quick, sending him a 'get lost' message in their every tap.

Furious still, although he was no longer there to see, she swung into her room, closing the door with a snapping click. Going into the shower room, she stripped and enjoyed the warm-to-cool cascade which sprayed all over her.

Seizing the towel, she wrapped it around her, easing back her damp hair and allowing it to hang loosely. The action lifted her chin and she gasped at the sight of the man standing, arms folded, ankles crossed, leaning against the shower room entrance. *How long had he been there?*

'This is my room,' she declared, pushing with the back of her hand at drops of water which clung to her mouth and eyes. 'Get out of it!'

'If you hadn't wanted me in here, you'd have locked the door,' he answered coolly.

'I did, I'm sure I did,' she snapped, realising to her annoyance that, although she had shut it with some force, she could not recall actually locking it.

'Would I be here if you had?'

It was a reasonable question, yet it annoyed her by its very reasonableness. 'So you're in the right and I'm in the wrong. You're in, but now will you please turn around,' she fixed the towel around her under the armpits, then pushed at him in her eagerness for him to be gone, 'and take yourself on your way.'

There was no moving him and she told herself she might as well be trying to manoeuvre a fully-grown elephant. He stayed right where he was.

'I was on my way,' he answered, taunting her with his smiling brown eyes, 'and I arrived at my destination. Here, in your bedroom. In reply, I might add, to that flashing look you gave me on your way up, which sent a very clear message, which was, "where I go will you please follow". I followed.'

Pushing still at his chest, she flared, 'It was a "get lost" look. I did not challenge you or invite you.'

He was as immovable as a mountain, and she panicked. His palms cupped her face, his thumbs stroked her softly pouting lips. His head lowered, but his mouth stayed poised while his eyes smiled into hers.

'Why are your lips trembling?' he asked. 'In anticipation—or fear?'

It was impossible to answer him, since it was both. Her hands pressed the towel to her, fearing its loosening would deprive her of her only barrier against him.

'Are you afraid?' His voice was deep and played a vibrant tune on her over-strung nerves. 'Of me?' he persisted.

This time she answered him. 'Yes, yes. Please, Zander, let me be.'

His response to her plea was to crush her in his arms, prising apart her yielding lips and tasting the very essence of her. She found her arms encircling his neck, her mouth accepting his as if it had every right to plunder it for treasure, and as if he had every right to be holding her as if she had promised to be his for ever.

Releasing her lips at last, he gazed into her bright eyes. It was as if he read a message there, one which Lisa was not even aware she was telling him. Holding her eyes, Zander moved. A moment later, she became conscious of the slow unwinding of the towel from her body. Hypnotised by the intensity of his gaze, she allowed the towel to fall away without a murmur of protest. At that moment, he could have done with her as he wanted.

He did not even touch her. It was his eyes again, deeply serious now, that traced a burning trail over her tingling skin. They lingered on the enticing thrust of her breasts, curved around her waist and hips, shading in the intimate femininity of her like an artist at work on a masterpiece.

'You're as beautiful as I imagined,' he said softly, then, bending, he retrieved the towel and slowly wound it round her. He spoke next from the door. 'Have your lunch, then meet me in the hotel foyer. I'll take you for a drive.'

He was there, waiting, when Lisa descended the stairs to the reception area. His welcome of her this time was more guarded, his gaze taking in the blue and white of her sundress and the way the bronze lights in her rich brown hair gleamed in the sunlight which shone through the glass doors.

Standing in front of him, she smiled up into his face. 'I obeyed your order,' she said, 'and I'm here, ready and waiting.'

He cupped her elbows, pulled her closer, 'And willing?'

Frowning, then smiling, she answered, 'No.'

'Och, woman, ye've go' a hard heart!' He had spoken with his broad Scottish accent, making her laugh again.

She shook her head. 'It's very soft, really.'

His eyes strayed downwards, lingered on the shape of her, then lifted. 'I could tell you to prove it.'

'You could,' she fenced, 'but I refuse to obey your *every* order. You might be boss where your colleagues are concerned, but you're not mine, Mr Cameron.'

His eyelids flickered, then were still. 'Come on outside and stop your blethering, as a Scotsman would say.'

Laughing again, Lisa followed him, taking his hand and looking at him to judge his reaction. He did not react, from which she deduced that if he had objected to having his hand seized by her, he would at once have withdrawn it.

They drove away from the town and into the

mysterious and brooding landscape of the island. 'I've never seen anything like this before!' Lisa exclaimed, straining forward in her effort to see everything it was possible to see and hoard the memories for future nostalgic inspection. 'Everywhere you look,' she went on, her gaze swinging from side to side, 'the ground's black just about as far as you can see. And it all looks so empty.'

'It's the emptiness my colleagues and I are here to fill,' Zander observed, driving as if he knew the terrain by heart.

'That's a terrible shame. Why don't the developers leave it alone,' she gestured broadly, 'all this grandeur, those secret mountains over there.'

'And where would you and your tourist friends stay when you visit the place?' Zander asked dryly. 'Sleep in tents on all that black dust? If it weren't for us, you probably wouldn't be here at all.' He manoeuvred the car to overtake a sightseeing coach. 'Incidentally, I find it ironic, to say the least, that you should be objecting to the new development. Didn't you know that Thistle International, the company you work for, is in on the construction business here, too?'

Lisa sank back, her eyes still taking in greedily the wild beauty of the environment. 'I did know, but only through Myra. She works for one of the department heads, whereas I work for Personnel. I deal with people, not projects. She suggested that we should come here for our holiday after hearing about the place from her boss.'

Zander smiled. 'So think next time before you criticise.'

Lisa sighed. 'I guess your logic in infallible, but it still doesn't stop me from criticising man's delight in desecrating beautiful places with only-too-visible reminders of his presence.'

'Point taken, Miss Maynard. It's as well you're not employed on the real work of the company that employs you.'

Annoyed, she turned to chide him, only to discover that he was smiling broadly. She settled back to enjoy the almost alien panorama of mountains and half-hidden valleys, of blue, near-cloudless skies and the distant haze of the sea.

'All this,' she lifted her hand, 'it's fascinating. It's like another planet. How did it happen?'

'Volcanic action. There's no water source and scarcely any rainfall, yet the island's inhabitants manage to grow vines and make wine from them. There are fig trees and citrus fruits. Maize, onions and tomatoes are coaxed from that incredible soil. At night, there's a heavy dew, and they've learned to make great use of that.'

'The people must work very hard,' Lisa commented, half to herself.

'They have to, to make a living, and against tremendous odds. In 1730, there was a series of devastating volcanic eruptions which went on for six years. There were more in the last century. That black lava you can see all around us came from those eruptions. It covered quite fertile soil.'

'But the people fought back?'

'With everything they'd got.'

There were villages now and then, with white, flat-roofed houses standing out brilliantly from the ash-grey of the surrounding lava. Here and there, between them stood a solitary palm tree, their great leaves moving constantly in the wind.

In the gardens of the houses, there were scarlet flowers or exotic cacti, small bushes and coddled and prized vegetables for use within the family. The fertility of the gardens contrasted dramatically with the black expanse of fields surrounding the villages.

'Volcanic ash contains useful minerals,' Zander commented, breaking into Lisa's reverie, 'which is why it's been scattered over the ground. It increases the growing power of the earth by helping to retain the moisture.'

Lisa nodded, spellbound by everything she saw. The sea was not far away now and they approached a settlement which gave shelter not to the island's inhabitants but to tourists.

'More property development,' Zander taunted, slowing to a stop. 'Do you disapprove of this, too?'

Looking around at the complex of apartments and villas which, it appeared, were filled with holidaymakers having the time of their lives, Lisa could only smile and shake her head. 'It looks fun. Swimming pools wherever I turn, a beach for the children to play on, sand that's really golden,' she glanced upwards, 'plus sunshine and yet more sunshine.' She sighed. 'It seems like heaven when you come from our kind of climate.'

Zander smiled into her eyes. 'So heaven is all around us. That's the effect you have on me.'

His statement, so full of meaning, yet spoken so rationally, toppled her off balance. What did he mean? Was he being serious? Did he want something from her? The questions ran nose to tail around her head.

Confused as to what was expected of her, she joked, 'You pay a pretty compliment, kind sir.'

'No compliment,' he stated, 'it's the truth.'

CHAPTER FOUR

EVEN as Lisa stared at him, she found he had gone serious on her. I'll never understand this man, she despaired. Staring ahead, she asked, 'Can we go back now?'

The day had gone dull, yet the sun shone just as brightly.

As they approached the hotel entrance after parking the car, Lisa enquired, 'Does your room overlook the sea?' He nodded, holding the door for her to enter. 'It's a pleasant room, then?'

'Pleasant enough.' He stopped, turning her to him. 'Are you hoping for an invitation?' Colouring, she shook her head. Why hadn't she realised how her questions must have sounded to him? 'Because,' he went on, 'you're not going to get one.'

Her cheeks flaming, she turned away. 'Please excuse me. Thanks for the drive and for putting up with my naïve company for the afternoon.'

He caught her arm. 'Climb down from your pedestal, woman. If I offended you, I'm sorry, but you must have known how a man—any man—would react to such questions.'

'Next time I'll know better.' She jerked free. 'If there is a next time.'

She made for the stairs and he joined her. 'Dine with me tonight.'

'I don't care if that's an order or an invitation. The answer's the same—no. Thank you.'

At the top of the stairs, he looked down at her, lifted his shoulders and walked away. In her room, Lisa flung herself into a chair. She was shaking now, with anger and disappointment.

Thank heaven, she thought, that Myra and Phil would be there to share the table. Then, when Zander entered with his colleagues, she would take pleasure in turning her back on him and talk and laugh with them. That way, she could hide her deep embarrassment at the way he had shaken off so casually her refusal of his invitation.

The meal went as she had planned. When he came in, she made a noisy move to the empty seat beside her, knowing that she had attracted Zander's attention. With her back to him, she made a play of enjoying Phil's jokes, laughing louder than Myra and, she congratulated herself, giving every appearance of having a wonderful time.

It was at the end of the meal, as they talked over coffee, that Phil persuaded his wife to go dancing that evening. 'Come with us,' Myra urged. 'Your bearded friend is sure to come looking for you. In fact, he's been staring at your back as if he'd like to wring your neck. Have you quarrelled with him or something?'

Lisa lifted her fast-tanning shoulders. 'He wanted me to dine with him—I refused. That's all.'

'That's all, for heaven's sake!' Phil exclaimed. 'No wonder he's giving you black looks. You must have hurt his pride.'

Lisa did not explain that it was the other way round—that he had hurt her pride. 'I won't come, thanks. You two go and enjoy yourselves. I'll write a few cards to friends.'

'Sure?' Myra asked as they were parting in the foyer. Lisa nodded emphatically, and her companions went on their way, holding hands.

Lisa did not write the cards as she had intended. Feeling restless, she stood on the balcony and watched the early evening swimmers below her on the beach. Soon she would join them, not in the sea but for a walk on the sands. First, while her meal was being digested, she would read.

It was, she discovered, easier to make the decision than to carry it out. The book she had bought was a good one, but this time it did not hold her attention. Lying on the bed instead of seated in a chair, she tried a magazine. For a while she flicked through it, enjoying the articles and one of the two short stories.

The restlessness surfaced again like a scuba diver who had had enough. Leave this room, it directed her, get out there, give your legs some work to do. She obeyed the feeling simply because it would not be denied, no matter how she fought against it.

The moment she swung from the bed, the telephone rang. Her heart leapt with her over-strung nerves and she gripped the receiver. 'Yes?' she asked.

'Will you dance with me?' The question came straight and confident, as if she were sitting at a table by the dance floor waiting for a partner. The low-pitched voice brought the owner's overwhelming sexiness into the room just as surely as if he were actually there beside her.

All the same, her answer was short. 'No, thanks. Find yourself another partner.' Lowering the receiver to its cradle, she clasped her hands between her knees and waited for the caller to ring again. There was nothing but silence. Perversely, she grew angry at his failure, for the second time that day, to persuade her to change her mind.

I'll swim, she thought, I'll change and go down there and plunge into that sea ... Seven minutes later she discovered just how cool the sea had grown with the sun gone down and nothing overhead to heat the atmosphere. But she didn't care, she told herself, gasping as she became fully immersed. For one moment she went under completely, then spurted upwards to gulp deep breaths and swim.

Striking out, she made for the now partly submerged rocks on which she had been sitting when one of Zander's colleagues had 'tested' her on his boss's behalf. The thought still had the power to anger, giving greater strength to her arm strokes and taking her skimming through the cool, calm sea.

'Mind those rocks!' The voice, through cupped hands for amplification, reached her ears. She recognised it but ignored its warning. He had not needed to warn, since she remembered their rough, cinder-like texture and the sharpness of their edges, formed as they had been by volcanic action.

In spite of this, as she clambered on to them in the fast-forming darkness, she grazed a leg. Peering in the half-light to inspect the wound, she was unaware of the swimmer who was also making for the rocks. It was not until he was climbing nimbly to avoid a similar abrasion to find a seat beside her that her irritation at his earlier offhandedness re-surfaced.

'Why did you bother to follow me out here?' she questioned, lowering her leg after discovering that she had not drawn blood. 'Had all the other women found themselves partners?'

'Who said I followed you? Maybe I just came for my own purposes—a swim, for instance, just as you did.'

'Then what are you doing sitting next to me?'

He eyed her with a faint touch of lust. 'You, with the figure of a young Venus, find it necessary to ask a man that?'

Her face grew warm, yet she dwelt deliberately on the outline of him, hoping to embarrass him in return. He smiled, tolerating her gaze. It took her a few moments to realise that her inspection had changed from a desire for revenge to one of intense appreciation of his muscled leanness, the strength and power of his build.

'Making sure I'm truly male?' he mocked. 'There's no need for me to reciprocate and assure myself of your femininity. It hits a man the moment he sees you.' He paused, eyeing her. 'Especially when you're dressed like that.'

On impulse, Lisa wriggled carefully down into the water, swam away from the reef and stumbled on to the shore. He was behind her immediately. Bending, she picked up her towel and rubbed herself down. He used his own smaller towel, dropped it, then took Lisa's towel from her clutching hands.

'I'm cold, Zander,' she protested, wrapping her arms around her. 'Please let me dry myself.' She could hardly see him in the darkness. The beach was empty now of other people. The hotel lights gave the only illumination and that did not stretch far.

He did not bother to answer, drying her instead with long, rough strokes. 'That's fine,' she declared, wishing

he would stop, since he left no part of her out, not
even where she was covered by the two-piece
swimsuit. The sensation of his touch, even through
the towel, was becoming too much to bear without
wanting to touch him back. 'My hair now,' she
added, 'I must dry that.'

At last the towel was returned and she lifted it to rub
at the long, damp strands which the wind was
gratuitously blowing dry. When Zander's hands
spanned her bare waist, she jumped, wishing she had
not demanded the towel back. The feel of his hands
without a barrier to protect her flesh was almost too
much to bear.

The towel dropped to the ground. He pulled her
down so that they were half lying on it. His arms slid
under her, one supporting her back, the other her head.
He shifted until he was partly her over, then brought
his mouth on to hers with a pressure that hurt—until
she parted her lips and allowed him entry.

Now she could not hold back from returning his
ardour. Her hands, which had rested on his shoulders,
slid upwards to rub through his damp hair. She found
her body moving with his, rolling on to their sides,
thigh to thigh, hip against hip. Only when she felt the
ruffled hairs on his chest brushing against her breasts
did she realise that he had removed her swimming top.

By then she was beyond caring. The palm of his hand
ran down the side of her body, over breast, waist and
hip, lingering there. He rolled her on to her back, his
hand over her throat, his kiss deepening until he seemed
to touch the very essence of her.

'My love, I want you.' The words came thickly
against her throat. 'Now I want you, do you hear?'

The sea broke in sighing waves, creeping up their
legs. The tide was coming in, but the fact did not
register on Lisa's singing mind. A half-moon had risen
high, stars glittered cleanly. The ocean was creeping
higher. Soon it would engulf them if they did not move.

'The tide—the tide, Zander!'

He seemed to drag himself back, but only halfway to
reality. 'Let it come in,' he mumbled against her breast,

'let it catch us and float us away, locked together to eternity.'

'Zander,' she said, urgently now, 'our things will get soaked and—and I'm cold, Zander.' A shiver ran through her and her trembling body in his arms returned him at once to the real world.

Lifting himself up, he pulled her with him. Lisa grabbed her towel before the sea had taken a single lap at it, dried her feet and pulled on her sandals. Smiling, she gestured to her bra top, asking him to fix it for her. Unsmiling, he obliged.

Now they were back to normal, his tender passion had left him. Only the throbbing of her lips and in her body the warm, dull ache for his love remained to remind her of all that had passed between them.

With her robe around her, she made her way up the beach and trod the steps into the hotel. Zander walked beside her, his shirt and jeans back in place. They took the lift, but they did not talk. His eyes were on her all the time, but she wondered if it was she he was really seeing.

Outside her room, she turned. 'Thanks for seeing me this far. Goodnight.'

He took the key from her hand, unlocked the door and motioned her inside.

Retreating, Lisa pushed out her hand, palm upwards. He had followed her in.

'You've still got my key,' she reminded, her smile uncertain.

He curled her fingers into the still-empty palm. 'I'll return it—when I've got what I want.'

Her eyes fell to hide her battling emotions. It was imperative that she did not let him see how much she wanted to indulge that 'want' of his. Everything within her was reaching out to him—her mind, her passions, her heart . . .

Horrified, she looked up at him. Had he perceived, even before she had guessed, what she had allowed herself so stupidly, so recklessly to do? Seemingly unperturbed, his eyes glittered down at her. Her eyelids fluttered closed for a passing second in thanks for his apparent failure to discover that, whether he wanted it or not, he was now in possession of her heart. A quiet voice added, And your love. Be honest.

His arm went round her waist, pulling her close. 'You haven't spoken, but I swear there's a lot going on inside this.' He tapped her head.

'Only because I'm thinking out the best way of saying that I'm sorry, but I—don't do that.'

Zander loosened his hold, seeming amused. 'Do what?'

His whole attitude disconcerted her. 'Give—give men what they want.'

He laughed, his face lighting up. She frowned, puzzled how any man could laugh when a woman had turned him down.

Fingers tipped up her face. 'Not even when all they want is a smile?'

Lisa laughed, a sense of relief fighting off a coating of disappointment.

'She laughed! Let me catch it.' His mouth opened as if to swallow hers, then the kiss grew serious, his arms wrapping round her slender form and encasing her as if she were lashed to him in a gale.

Her hands moved from his shoulders to curl around his neck. When he pressed her to him, she went, delighting in the muscled thighs pushing against hers, his hips making indentations on her soft ones. Breathless when he raised his head, she smiled into the brown eyes, which told of his pleasure, yet also of an unfulfilled need.

'What will you do with my laughter?' she joked. 'Take a whole page in your book and give it more space than your "kiss stamps"?'

His eyes grew thoughtful. 'I'll do better. I'll tape it and play it back in my low and lonely moments.'

'Lonely? Do you really not have a wife?'

For a moment he grew distant, as if he were not there, but in some other place. The seriousness of his expression put worry into her eyes, then he was back with her, a smile lifting the corners of his mouth.

'I don't have a wife.' He paused at the door, 'Goodnight, Lisa.'

She ran across to him. She was determined to ask, even if convention dictated that she should not. 'Tomorrow I suppose you'll be working?'

He flicked her cheek lightly. 'For a change, I shall be playing. Touring the island, in fact. With a female companion.'

Lisa was so disappointed, she could have cried. Turning away, she remarked as lightly as she could, 'I see.'

He turned her back. 'You don't see. The female will be you.'

Her pleasure was so transparent, he would have had to be blind not to see it, but she did not care. 'I'll be ready. What time?'

'Mid-morning. I'll see you around in the foyer, hm?'

Nodding, she answered, 'In the foyer.'

Zander bent his head and brushed her lips with his. 'Don't look so disgustingly pleased with the idea! Man is traditionally the hunter, woman the hunted.' He whispered against her ear, 'Just as long as when I chase you and you start running, you run towards me.'

Her hand reached up and tugged his beard. He slapped her hand playfully, then put it to his lips. She watched him walk away.

Over breakfast, Lisa explained to Myra and Phil that she would be spending the day with Zander.

'So you've discovered him at last—that special man you were looking for, I mean,' Myra commented, smiling at her husband as he took her hand in his. It was a possessive 'you're mine, remember,' gesture which Lisa found touching.

Her shoulder lifted and she pushed away her empty coffee cup. 'Maybe. But it's of no significance, is it? I mean, at the end of our time here, that's it. I won't see him again. He's a wanderer, he told me so.'

Phil looked up quickly, past Lisa. A wary look took over, causing him to release his wife's hand selfconsciously. Zander was standing beside Lisa now, smiling, relaxed, his cream-coloured shirt opened at the neck, his belted slacks a deep brown and well-fitting.

Lisa's heartbeats speeded, her face grew pink. Had he heard the conversation? He nodded to Myra and Phil, exchanging a few words with them as if they were all equals. Yet, in her heart, Lisa knew instinctively that Zander Cameron was not their equal, either in status or background.

'Finished your breakfast?' Zander enquired. Lisa nodded. 'Coming?' he pursued. Lisa nodded again, rising. Always nodding at him, she thought bemusedly, always doing exactly as he wants. Did he realise how much power he wielded over her?

'She hasn't eaten enough to satisfy a mouse,' Phil commented.

'I think she's pining,' Myra added mischievously. Lisa gave her a dark look and Myra pretended to hide her face.

Zander laughed, seeming amused by Lisa's irritation. As they walked away he took her hand. 'So I'm the "special" man you've been looking for? That's good to know.'

Lisa nodded, falsely wise. 'Your pride finds it nice to know, I have no doubt.'

They were outside now and approaching the hotel's car park. 'If there were not so many people around,' Zander asserted, his voice low, 'I'd spank you for that.'

As she settled herself in the passenger seat, she retorted, 'Of course your pride's flattered. How could it be anything else? For us, as we agreed, there are no yesterdays and no tomorrows, which leaves only today.'

'Make the most of today,' he counselled, joining the road and driving away from the town. 'Tomorrow will soon be here.'

Lisa's eyes closed against the sun's brilliance, shutting out, too, the strangely beautiful landscape in which they were now driving. How could she appreciate anything which this curiously fascinating island had to offer now she knew this man beside her had reminded her of how short their time together would be?

'My camera—I meant to bring my camera!' Her eyes, blue, intense and sad, found his. 'What shall I do?'

'I have mine,' he answered offhandedly, 'there on the

back seat. Whatever picture you want me to take, just tell me.' His brief smile was in direct contrast to her turned-down mouth. 'Give me your address and I'll send you copies.'

Agreeing with a nod, her heart lifted at the thought that the link with him would not be entirely broken. Then she knew the idea was impossible. After today, their lives would never touch again. Silently she decided to 'forget' to give him her address. A clean break would be imperative. What use was there in prolonging the agony?

'Where are we going?' she asked, finding a certain contentment in the decision she had arrived at.

'Wherever the car decides to take us.'

Lisa watched his tanned arms, dark with hair, controlling the steering wheel, the muscles revealing a toughness which, she guessed, was inherent in his nature, yet which he had so far chosen to keep under wraps for the duration of his acquaintance with her.

Watching the beaches from the car, Lisa noticed how empty they were and how some were covered in black volcanic ash, while other parts were like golden sand.

'We're turning away from the coast now,' Zander informed her, 'and making for the interior.'

'It looks even more fantastic each time I see it,' Lisa commented. 'There's blackness everywhere, instead of the brown earth we see at home.'

'That ash has been put there by the farmers,' Zander explained. 'They spread it over soil in which the crops are sown.'

'You mean it helps them grow?'

'It protects them from the wind, for a start. It also retains whatever moisture there may be in the atmosphere. You can guess how important that is,' Zander enlarged, 'in a place where, as I said, there's no water source and scarcely any rainfall.'

'How did you learn all this?' Lisa turned admiring eyes to him.

Glancing at her briefly, he laughed. 'In my job, I make it my business to know these things. But any courier taking a coachload of tourists around will give you this information.

'So I have my own personal courier.' Lisa's smile was provocative.

'I put up my charges for cheeky tourists,' he replied blandly, at which Lisa smiled again.

The black ground became interspersed with patches of green. They climbed to the top of the hills and Lisa exclaimed at the sight of them.

'These are the island's vineyards,' Zander explained. 'Yes, I know it's hard to believe that vines grow here, but it's only because of the islanders' dedication to their land.'

The lava and black sand had been fashioned into hollows with small semi-circular walls of rock to protect each vine. 'The hollows,' Zander explained, 'encourage the dew to linger, and capture any rain which might fall. It collects in the sunken bowl of ash and the plants thrive on it.'

Zander drew up at a wine lodge. This was again a white-painted building, its windows shuttered. Tall cacti and trees grew upwards from the black ground at the building's front.

Lisa followed Zander down a steep, gravelled slope and into a large, dark room where they were welcomed by smiling people. 'You can have as many glasses of the wine as you want,' Zander told her with a glint in his eye. 'Just as long as I don't have to carry you out of here in a drunken stupor.'

'It's very sweet,' Lisa commented, tasting her sample, 'and it's going to my head, I can feel it.'

Zander drained his glass and took Lisa's empty glass from her. 'That's it,' he declared, 'otherwise I can see you won't be able to walk out on your own two feet!'

They drove on past salt works where wind pumps raised the sea water into shallow pans. 'After evaporation,' Zander told her, 'deposits of salt are left and raked into large pyramids. There's also a desalination plant. Now that tourism here is growing, that became an absolute necessity,' he added.

Around them, the landscape changed yet again. It

was, Zander explained, the volcanic zone. Lisa saw with astonished eyes the way the mountains had changed from black to blending shades of pink, red and green, stretching into the far distance.

'Soon,' Zander explained, 'we'll be in the region of the Montañas del Fuego, the Mountains of Fire.'

On the way, and in the distance, they saw two camel trains snaking their slow way up one of the steep and dusty mountainsides. Tourists were carried in chairs slung, two by two, across the dromedaries' backs, while guides escorted them.

The car drew up near the base of a slope. Zander invited Lisa to get out and feel the wind in her face. This she did, dipping her head against the gusts. They lunched in the circular restaurant which had been built especially for tourists. The food was good, while on the table wine and mineral water stood ready.

Glad just to be with Zander, Lisa took every moment in her two hands and squeezed each one dry of happiness. The past was safe in her memory, the future an infinite blank. All she had was now—the present, living and breathing, linking them until the holiday's end did them part.

Outside again, Zander took every shot she asked for. In the restaurant, he had captured the view through the full-length windows. It stretched from the dry brush-wood in the foreground to the black lava which ended in a dark beach of ash.

In the distance was the sea, its deep blue edged with white spray. Lisa could only stare with a mixture of pleasure and awe at the alien yet incomparably beautiful panorama which spread all around them.

All the time the wind blew and dust and particles of rock stung Lisa's legs. Zander crouched down to ease away her pain, his massaging hands cool yet making her skin burn wherever he touched her. His hand moved higher to hold still her inner thigh and a shudder of excitement ran through her. He looked up, eyebrows raised, a small smile pulling at his mouth. He knew what he was doing to her!

As he straightened, there was the sound of other

vehicles arriving. Two coaches unloaded their passen-
gers, who swarmed in all directions. They appeared to
be as awe-stricken by their surroundings as Lisa had
been. There was a shout and groups drifted towards a
man who stood nearby at the side of a hole which had
been dug into the ground.

With people gathered around him, he threw a piece
of dry brushwood into the hole. Immediately, smoke
rose from it and the brushwood burst into flames. The
heat was sufficient to make people recoil as the wind
blew the smoke and dancing flames in their direction.

'That,' said Zander, 'demonstrates how hot the
ground is beneath our feet.' Others were listening to
him now, as if he were a guide.

'How far under our feet?' a man enquired.

'Roughly sixty centimetres, or at just under two feet,
the temperature reaches about four hundred degrees
centigrade, that is,' Zander did a rough mental
calculation, 'around eight hundred to nine hundred
degrees Fahrenheit.'

People gasped and looked down at their feet,
laughing as they tried to find evidence of their sandals
melting. Zander's arm around Lisa's waist propelled her
from the crowd to a quieter area. They scuffed through
pink-shaded sand and grey ash towards a wall made of
volcanic, cinder-like rock.

He eased her round to face him. 'Beautiful though
this strange landscape is,' Zander pronounced, 'there's
something even more beautiful missing from the day.'
He smiled at her puzzled frown. 'Shall I demonstrate?'

He took his kiss. When he would have broken away,
her arms held fast to him and she gave him back her
own kiss in exchange. His eyes were bright and when
the brightness faded, they held a look she could not
decipher. Never again, she told herself, would she be as
happy as she was today.

'We haven't taken any pictures of ourselves,' Zander
remarked, opening his camera case. 'That must be
remedied.'

'Me first,' Lisa claimed, her hand outstretched. He
lifted the camera and snapped her, at which she

protested loudly. Going across to him, she tried to prise his fingers away from the camera, but he stopped her sharply.

Moving a few paces, she showed her pain at his abruptness, and he laughed. 'You look like a dog with its ears down! I didn't mean to bark, but this piece of equipment was expensive. You also need to be shown how to use it.'

At once her face cleared. The man she had come to know had returned.

'Show me,' she demanded, going close to him. And he did, telling her exactly how to hold it.

Standing at the stated distance, she trained the camera on to him. She saw him, for a frightening second, as the camera would not see him—in a suit of grey, with an air of authority, unapproachable and cold. Hurriedly removing the camera from her eye, she stared at him to reassure herself that the picture she had seen had been her imagination playing tricks, affected by the wine they had drunk, the beating heat of the sun and the driving wind playing havoc.

'Now what's wrong?' Zander demanded.

'Nothing,' she replied airily, 'just taking my time, like all true artists.'

His smile was broad at her answer. Still she held until the smile had started to fade. Then she clicked and he was there inside the camera. When he sent them to her—and something told her he would keep his word—she would be able to hold the picture to her, sleep with it framed beside her bed.

Walking back to him, she glimpsed a wildness about him, of a passion leashed, of pleasure released in tiny doses like a medicine taken only once a day. Everything about him was on a tight rein—the movement of muscle in his thighs, the strength his arms possessed as they rested on his hips as he waited for her to return his camera.

'I hope,' he commented, 'your examination of me reassured you that I came up to your high standards.' He accepted his camera, slinging it across his shoulder. Grasping her arm, he asserted, 'I think I should repay the compliment and let my eyes explore you.'

'I wish,' she interposed, diverting him hastily, 'we had a picture of us together.'

'That shouldn't be difficult.' Zander gazed around, seeing the father of a young family standing nearby. He approached the man, exchanged a few words and the man nodded. Walking over, he listened as Zander explained the workings of his camera, taking it and handling it carefully.

The man smiled and nodded to Lisa, who smiled back. Zander pushed his hand around her waist, whispered, 'Say "cheese",' at which Lisa laughed. The camera clicked.

'Another one?' the young father asked, and caught them as Lisa's head rested momentarily on Zander's shoulder.

'No,' Lisa protested, 'scrub that out!'

Zander laughed, swung her round and caught her in his arms, kissing her forcefully. The camera clicked again. They drew apart, Lisa's mouth open to protest more strongly, when she saw that it was not the father who had taken the photograph.

The man holding the camera was Zander's fair-haired colleague.

CHAPTER FIVE

ZANDER almost pushed her from him, the line of his lips tight as he strode across to the man. A few words passed, then the man walked away, a faintly indolent air about him.

Zander's face was thunderous as he replaced his camera in its case.

'Something wrong?' Lisa asked, puzzled and showing it.

'Nothing that need worry you.' His offhandedness must have reverberated back at him, since his manner changed. 'Colleagues sometimes overstep the mark,' was his enigmatic reply.

'Especially when they annoy the boss,' Lisa dared, sighing thankfully when he smiled.

He caught her hand, swinging it between them lightly. 'Next stop, the Jameo del Agua. *Jameos* are places where the ground has sunk. They are, I'm told, called *malpais*, that is, modern lava zone.'

Tourists were everywhere when they arrived. Zander explained that this *jameo* was the most famous. 'It has a subterranean lagoon where, they say, a unique species of albino crab lives. Whatever you do,' he warned, 'walk carefully. Incidentally,' he added, 'there's a night club accommodated here.'

'To which you've been, no doubt,' Lisa remarked, smiling provocatively.

He slanted a glance at her. 'Since you seem to have decided that I have, there's no need for me to answer, is there?'

They were within reach of the coast, Lisa discovered, gazing round. The car was parked by a beach of brown rock which was scattered with green lichen. A guide attached to a group of people from a touring coach was explaining the formation of the cave.

'It was,' she said, in excellent English, 'formed by a

hollow tube of lava which ran into the sea. In the pool lives an extremely rare species of blind white crabs, unique to this lake, about the size of a thumbnail.'

There were exclamations of amazement from the group, and even Lisa examined her thumbnail, making Zander laugh and seize her hand. 'Let's go inside,' he said, leading her through an archway and to the top of steep, curving steps.

Lisa caught her breath at the sight that greeted them. They were looking at a rich garden, where the cacti reached upward, way above their heads, tall as a tree.

'About thirty feet high, I should think,' Zander estimated.

Plants, bushes, trees and exotic flowers of every kind and colour wound themselves around the spiral stone staircase which led to a pool.

Reflected in it was the image of a similarly lush garden from the other end of the cavern. In the centre of the rock ceiling was a hole letting in daylight, and Lisa saw that the rock forming the cavern's ceiling was a light pink.

Hidden lighting had been used to great effect and soft music played through speakers, intensified the romantic atmosphere and the impact the whole place had on the onlooker. On a plateau, built into a natural alcove, was a bar. Tables and chairs stood waiting to be occupied.

Zander seized Lisa's hand as they walked beside the pool. It was dark and the path narrow. Other people passed constantly. At the bottom of the pool there were hundreds of shining coins. Lisa noticed, after walking further into the cave's darkness, that the coins shone like a million stars in the velvet depths of the water.

Zander's arm went quickly round her waist. 'You went too near. It must be having an hypnotic effect on you,' he remarked, a note of anxiety in his tone.

'Like you do on me,' Lisa answered, laughing up into his eyes. Had her laughter hidden from him the truth in her statement? In the cave's mysterious half-light, she could not judge his reaction.

After a drink at the bar, they left the cool magic of

the place. Lisa knew that she would never forget its awesome beauty.

'Come on,' said Zander as Lisa turned away from the wind's breathtaking impact, 'let's go home.'

Still under the spell of the cave, she frowned, asking, 'Home?' Then reality faded in and she replied, 'Home is a long way.'

'Anywhere is home when you're there, too,' he returned incomprehensibly.

Dinner was over and Zander had suggested a walk on the hotel's private beach. He'll never know, Lisa reflected, as they walked hand in hand down the paved slope to the golden sand, that I'd go with him to the end of the earth and back, if he asked me.

On the way out, they had passed Zander's colleague. It seemed that Zander had not yet forgiven the man for taking the photograph back at the restaurant, since his nod was curt. The man had responded by throwing a smile at Lisa which bordered on insolence.

Zander's arm, which had been round her waist, had tightened until it hurt as he witnessed the man's leer. Questioningly, Lisa had sought Zander's face for an explanation, but none had come.

They were on the sands now, glowing in the lowering sun. 'What's that man's name?' she asked.

'Reg Beckley. Twice divorced and looking out for a replacement woman.'

'You sent him down to test me,' she accused.

'On the contrary,' he was retreating from her, his grip on her hand easing, 'he came of his own accord. For his own purposes.'

Lisa smiled up at her companion, gripping his hand so that it did not slip away. 'I told him where he could go—in a very ladylike way, of course!'

Zander laughed and Lisa joined in. I've got him back again, she thought with immense relief, I've stopped his retreat. This evening he had dressed more formally in suit and tie. The sight of him like that irritated her, reminding her of working life, the busy streets of London, the suited-and-tied business men wrapped in their own particular worlds of overseas calls, meetings and conferences.

Halting him, she put the flat of her hands on his jacket, searching his eyes for a reprimand. Finding none, she let her fingers walk upward to his tie. Smiling, she loosened it, then stopped. The only reaction from him was a smile in return. Finally she removed the tie, rolled it and pushed it into his pocket, then reached up to unfasten the first two shirt buttons.

Moving back a pace, she asked, 'Did you mind?'

'If I had, cheeky minx, I'd have let you know the moment you started.'

'That's what I thought.' She unfastened another button. 'There, that's better. You look more relaxed now.'

Zander put his hand to the rounded neckline of her dress. 'I've an urge to return the compliment.' His fingers started to unfasten the top button of her sleeveless floral-print dress.

'What are you doing?' She clapped her hands over his.

'Giving you a plunge neckline.' His smile was wicked. 'On the other hand, why should I stop there? If I undo the buttons all the way, you'll look more relaxed, too.'

'Oh, no,' she gripped his hand and pulled it away. 'I'm wearing—very little underneath.'

His hand escaped her hold and returned to her dress. 'All the more reason . . .' Her hands stilled his wrist. His eyes dropped to her mouth. 'You're adorable,' he said, and took her lips in a kiss. When he stopped, Lisa held up her mouth for another. Laughing indulgently, he gave her a second one.

His arm found her waist again and hers lifted to his, under his jacket. They made footprints in the wet sand near the water's edge. A couple sat on a sloping reef of brown rocks. A rowing boat was beached, oars left carelessly. A red lounger reclined emptily near the steps.

Lisa liked the feel of the man walking beside her. She liked the height of him, the darkness of his hair, the feel of his thighs moving against hers. His brown eyes held secrets she knew she would never be told and behind the black bush of beard and moustache was a face he had insisted she wouldn't like.

Like? she thought, lowering her head to his shoulder and loving the firmness she found there; I love everything about him. It was, she acknowledged, a love without hope of fulfilment, but surely, she argued, it didn't hurt anyone to love another person. It could only enrich them, couldn't it? She closed her mind to the pain she would feel the day she would have to say goodbye to him.

'You've drifted,' he declared, pulling her closer to his side. Strange, she reflected, how he seems to sense my mental absence, just as I sense his. 'I've lost you in your thoughts. What were they?'

Lisa lifted a shoulder. 'Of no consequence, really. Except——' an idea darted in, 'except I'm wondering what ingredients you think a marriage should have to make it work, really work?'

'You tell me.' He turned her to face him. They were standing on the shaded side of a reef which climbed the beach out of the sea. The sun was sinking fast and the wind blew strongly, tossing hair and pulling at clothes.

'Well,' she put her head on one side, 'there's laughter and, of course, friendship, as I said before.'

'So love,' he put in, 'comes a long way down your list of priorities in a relationship between a man and a woman?'

'Ah, love . . . now that is something else entirely. Don and I made love.'

His eyes flickered, then narrowed. 'Tell me what you call making love.'

'Well, we kissed and——' Her eyes defied him. 'I don't see why I should go into details. We——' Her smile returned. 'We didn't go all the way.' His mouth had softened from its hardened line. 'Only until I said "stop".'

He pretended to look horrified. 'My dear,' he groaned, 'my guts ache in sympathy with his agony!'

Lisa laughed, her head thrown back, her brown curling hair blowing round her face.

A gust of wind, particularly strong, blew across the

bay, picking up sand and pelting them with it. It caught
Lisa on every exposed part of her skin, stinging her
cheeks and prickling her eyes.

'Oh!' She gave a strangled gasp and flung her arm
across her face, protecting it. Zander turned quickly from
his involuntary swivel from the wind's force. He pulled
a handkerchief from his pocket and encircled her waist,
wiping her face and smoothing the sand from her eyes.

'Blink hard,' he instructed, then helped her rid her
eyelids of the dust.

After a moment, he asked, 'Okay now?'

Lisa nodded, looking up at him and smiling a watery
smile, her eyes moist from tears which had risen to
cleanse them. It was dark now and they could only see
each other with the aid of the hotel's lights. Her smile
faded when she saw how serious he had become.

He held her under the armpits, drawing her towards
him. They were touching now, her soft breasts against
his wall of chest, her hips and thighs compressed by the
angles and rigidity of his. In the semi-darkness, she
strained to discern his mood, for his hold on her seemed
almost angry.

'I want you,' he said roughly, his voice so low the
breaking waves almost overcame the sound, 'my love, I
want you!' She was silent, since her heart was pounding
so hard she could not utter a word. 'Answer me, damn
you, why don't you tell me to go to hell?'

'Because I——' she managed, then her head fell to his
chest, 'I want you, too.' Only then did he let her know
of his increasing desire. After a moment of forbidden
delight that he should need her so, she eased away,
although still in his arms, which were wrapped about
her slender body as if he would never release her. She
lifted her head. 'I never have, Zander, but if you want
me?'

The statement ended as a question, for she was as
much out of her depth now as if she were in fact
floundering in that vast and empty sea out there.

'Tonight,' he muttered, and she saw his eyes were
closed, 'it must be tonight.' He was looking at her now.
'Tomorrow I'll be gone.'

Dazed, she broke away and stared out at the sea she could hear but scarcely see. The tide was ebbing, like the ocean of happiness in which she had been floating since morning. Had she somehow sensed that this would be the final day?

Their last day together ... Her heart drummed on, but it hammered out a message of despair. How could she face the remaining time of the vacation, the empty, far-reaching years of her life, without him?

How deeply she had fallen in love with this man she had not realised until that moment. Slowly she turned, seeing his dark outline defined by the lights. His hands were in his pockets. His gaze was on her. She could feel it as well as guess it from the stillness of his body.

Walking back to him, Lisa put her palms on his chest and rested her cheek between them. She felt the expansion and contraction as he breathed, heard the fast heartbeat. Her arms slipped down to hold him round her waist. His hands stayed where they were.

'I've done something unforgivable.' Her voice trembled. 'I've fallen in love on holiday. With you, Zander, with you.' For a few seconds, he seemed almost to have stopped breathing, then the rising and falling of her head began again. 'But it doesn't matter. You see, I know this is the end of things, now you're going. You can forget I ever said it. And I—I'll attach no real importance to it at all. I'll force myself to forget you, like I made myself forget Don.' She looked up at him, but his face was in complete shadow. 'I'll get over it.'

Without warning, the tears welled and spilled. Zander moved at last, cradling her, rocking her gently. The wind blew in great gusts, as if trying to tear them apart. The waves seemed to have grown louder, although they had moved away. Sand swirled about them, but still he held her.

Someone laughed, and there were footsteps descending from the hotel to the beach. Zander and Lisa moved apart as the group of young people approached, noisy in their delight at being young and on holiday and attacked by dust and gusts.

The pressure of Zander's hand on Lisa's back urged her towards the hotel. In the lift, they stood apart, Zander leaning against a mirror as he read the Spanish words of the advertisements. Lisa smoothed her hair, shaking out the sand.

He escorted her to the door of her room. He took the key, motioned her in, returned the key. She waited for his polite but regretful farewell. Instead, he followed her in, switching on the concealed lighting.

'Zander?' she whispered, wanting to run to him and shake him until his stiff figure loosened, allowing him to smile. He didn't smile, not even when he walked towards her.

His fingers pressed her cheeks as he held her face, tipping it upward. 'I want to spend the night with you in my arms.'

The blue of her eyes deepened, mixing with his brown. 'You're tearing me apart, Zander, especially after what I told you.'

'I want to feel you there beside me, once, just once in the whole of our lives.' There was a low-pitched urgency in his voice that caught at her inner being.

All along, she had known she would agree, but even now she must not let him guess the fact, must not let him think she was so easy to get.

'Will you give me time? While I prepare for bed, I'll think, then think again. And when you come back, I'll tell you.'

His hands dropped away, leaving her mouth unkissed. It felt parched and discarded. He took the key she offered him. When he went through the door, he did not look back.

For a long time she stood at the balcony window. It was closed, but she was sure she could hear the sigh of the waves. Turning, she prepared for bed, conscious of a feeling of inevitability, of her destiny so soon to be fulfilled—then passed by and left at the wayside.

By the time he returned, she wore her filmy calf-length nightdress, covered by a matching gown. It lifted and fell in the breeze as she turned to greet him. He wore a towelling robe. His hair was touch-damp from a shower, his beard similarly so.

His eyes reached her first, running over her, appreciating every curve, every shapely part of her. Then he was there, feathering her hair with his fingers, touching her cheeks, her throat. The gown was being removed. It fell to the floor.

He eased down the shoulder of her nightdress, first trailing the silkiness of her skin with the pads of his fingertips, following his tactile exploration with feathering caresses of his mouth. When his hand cupped a breast, and his head bent to kiss it to throbbing life, her head hung back in her joy at the intimacy.

The nightdress slipped from her entirely to rest in a pile on the carpet, but she was beyond caring. Zander had seen her naked before, but he had not touched her. Now he was inflaming her desires with the strength of his, and when he scooped her up at last and carried her to the bed, her eyes fluttered open to see that he had shed his robe. He was not entirely unclothed, since his underpants were still in place.

Hazily, she wondered whether he had not discarded them out of consideration for her sensibilities. She managed a smile. 'I'm not ignorant of a man's anatomy,' she whispered. 'I've seen photographs in magazines——'

For a moment, his eyes had darkened. Now he threw himself beside her and stopped her flow of words with his mouth, prising open her lips with the force of his own. The rest of her he gathered to him, letting her feel his arousal, skimming her flesh with his palm, seeking out unviolated places and making her feel and accept the overwhelming masculinity of him.

Her arms clung, then moved, never still for long, stroking his back, enjoying the rough friction of his chest hair against her breasts. Her hand smoothed over his hair, running round to his face and, in her pleasure, tugging at tufts of his beard. The kiss was over and she lay there eagerly awaiting its renewal.

When at last he moved on to her, her entire body throbbed with longing for him. He held back and she wondered if he was waiting for a sign of acquiescence from her.

'Yes, oh yes,' she whispered, arching to him. Still he made no move to take her. How could she say to him, I'm aching for you to become my lover, because I love you so very much?

'No, oh no,' he answered smiling, and mockery was not far away. He kissed away her frown. 'I said I wanted to spend the night with you in my arms. One thing I will not do, my sweet girl, is take away your innocence. If you allow another man to do so, that's for you to decide. Me,' he ran a hand down her side to her hips, 'I'm stopping right here. Before you give that dreaded command,' he said with a smile, 'such as you told me you gave your ex-boy-friend. Also, I'm stopping to save my own agony of body, not to mention my mind.'

'Zander,' her fingers made dents in his tanned, hard shoulders, 'I'd never command you to stop, not you, of all men. I——' She turned away, trying to control her quivering lip. 'Tomorrow you're leaving. I'll never see you again.'

He went back on to his side, his hand stroking her cheek, moving down to hold her breast, caressing it with his thumb. 'Just suppose there were—consequences. Just imagine how you—and I—would feel.'

'I'd never tell you,' she countered fiercely, 'I'd never worry you with the problem. It would be mine——'

'And my child.'

'Anyway, you're a wanderer, you told me. I wouldn't even know where you were. So I couldn't tell you.'

His hand was arousing her and she rolled towards him. His head lowered to kiss the shape he had been caressing, then he urged her against him.

'I'll hold you.' He pressed her cheek against his chest and she moved his beard to one side, the better to hear the heart of him. 'Remember what Robert Burns said?' he asked against her hair. '"Know prudent cautious self-control is wisdom's root".' Her head moved so that she could look up into his face. 'You'll remember me, my bonnie dearie, as the man who held back of his own accord, without your embargo being placed on him first. Now pull the covers over us while I switch out the lights.'

When they had settled down at last, the sigh that came from her was from her very depths. The excitement and passion he had brought to life within her was dying down. She was safe, and strangely satisfied, in his arms.

'You ought,' she murmured, near to sleep, 'to shave off your beard. All that hair—I can't see you properly, the real you.'

'I'll do that, my Lisa, I'll shave it off, I swear. But I warn you again, you'll regret the consequences.'

In the morning, Zander left her early. He pulled on his robe and tied it.

Bending over her as she lay, sleepy-eyed, he said, 'I'll quote Robbie Burns again. "Ae fond kiss, and then we sever".'

I don't want to sever from you, her mind cried in anguish. I want you to stay with me for ever. Her lips never spoke the words.

He gathered her to him, lifting her as he sat sideways on the bed. She felt no embarrassment now at his seeing her naked. Weren't they lovers, although their lovemaking was incomplete?

He kissed her with a passion that drew a heat into her limbs. Overwhelmed by the ease with which he coaxed her desire into being, Lisa returned his passion and more. In those moments, she gave herself into his memory's keeping.

I love you, she wanted to cry, as her tormented eyes followed him to the door.

'Will you smile at me?' he asked.

Her smile at his bidding flooded her face, but she could not prevent it from wavering.

For a moment he gazed back at her. Then he was gone.

Slipping into sleep again, Lisa awoke late, missing breakfast. It didn't matter, she told herself, since she wasn't hungry. She didn't think she would ever be hungry again.

The internal telephone rang as she tidied her belongings. She jumped, her hand shot out, then she told herself not to allow her imagination to get the better of her common sense.

'Myra?' said Lisa. 'Yes, I missed breakfast. Overslept? Maybe, but I just wasn't hungry.'

'What's going on with you and your Zander?' Myra queried. 'The bird has flown, to coin a phrase. Did you know? Phil and I were sitting in the foyer waiting for you when who should come down the stairs, all dressed for business and no-nonsense, but Mr Cameron.'

'Did he see you?'

'He stared at us. Seemed to be searching for someone. I wonder who that was?' Myra added dryly. 'Anyway, he was carrying a couple of suitcases and seemed to be in a hurry. He looked like a real live executive.'

'Did he say anything?' Lisa asked with a touch of wistfulness.

'He was in too much of a hurry to talk to mere nothings like Phil and me. He did nod, though, and called out that he wished us every happiness.'

And me, Lisa thought, a lump in her throat, every unhappiness.

'What's wrong?' Myra asked, sounding concerned. 'Didn't you know he was leaving?'

'Yes, I knew.' She must have sounded choked, since Myra urged,

'Have a good cry, dear. Take Aunty Myra's advice— let it all come out. It was only a holiday romance, after all, and they never last, do they?'

Lisa was glad that Myra could not see her face. She agreed, even nodding her head, probably in an effort to convince herself. Arranging to meet them later, she rang off, covering her face. Zander had said, You'll remember me as the man who held back of his own accord. He was as good as his word. All night he had held her, but he had not made love. His restraint still puzzled her. If he was really a man who roamed the world, and she saw no reason to doubt him, why had he not taken her and said to hell with the consequences?

Going down in the lift, Lisa looked around for her friends. They were missing, and again she found herself waiting. Staring out at the tourists seated in the coaches drawn up outside, and at the guests entering and leaving through the glass doors, she did not see the man who was approaching.

Only when she felt the occupation of the other half of the two-seater couch did she surface from her melancholy thoughts and face the newcomer. His hair was fair, his expression unpleasant.

'Mourning your lost lover?' he asked.

If it had not been for the circumstances, she would have taken exception to the absence of respect in his tone. 'What do you mean?' she returned sharply.

'You know what I mean. Mr Zander Cameron. I'd advise you to forget him, sweetie.'

'Why?' She had paled now and her tormentor seemed to be enjoying her uneasiness.

'Why? Because he's engaged to be married, that's why.'

'You mean he's got a girl waiting for him back home?'

'I mean he's got a girl waiting. She wears his ring, diamonds and emerald. He's a wealthy guy, is Z. Cameron. So, as I said, forget him. He's way beyond your reach.'

CHAPTER SIX

THE journey home was almost over. For much of the flight, Lisa had pretended to read a magazine. Myra and Phil had been solicitous and understanding, especially when she had told them that Zander had, all the time, been engaged.

'Did it really and truly matter, though?' Myra had asked. 'You won't be seeing him ever again, will you? Just as long as——' she had looked quickly at Lisa, then away, 'you didn't do anything you—well, might regret. In the future, I mean.'

Lisa had assured her that she had not, at which Myra had looked deeply relieved. Except, Lisa had thought, lost my heart in its entirety to a total stranger.

The remainder of the holiday Lisa had spent on the beach in the bay. Sometimes Myra and Phil had been there, too, but at other times, they had gone sightseeing, while she stayed there alone. Lying full-length and just listening to the waves had taken her floating back into Zander's arms as they had made love that wonderful night, while the tide had lapped at their feet.

Most evenings, Myra and Phil had danced. Lisa had sat at the table watching them. Once, Zander's colleague, the fair-haired man who had so bluntly broken the news of Zander's engagement, had joined her.

'I'll take his place,' Reg Beckley had offered, slicking back his blond hair.

'Don't tell me,' Lisa had answered sharply, 'you need a woman in your life, having shed two wives.'

'I see our friend Cameron has been telling tales.'

'I doubt if you swore him to secrecy, which means he was telling the truth with impunity.'

He gave her a glance she did not like, then drew out a packet of cigarettes, offering it to her.

'I don't smoke, thanks, and——' as he went to take

one for himself, 'I'd be glad if you didn't either, in my presence.'

Lifting his shoulders carelessly, he had slid the packet away. His eyes had wandered to the couples moving round in the semi-darkness. 'Dance?' he'd asked.

Lisa had shaken her head, clutching her bag—the same bag Zander had put into his jacket pocket as it had been draped round that exact seat.

'Look, Lisa——'

'Don't call me Lisa!'

He smiled at her sharpness. 'Okay, Miss Maynard, then.' Lisa knew she had been churlish, but her name spoken by him had jarred her taut nerves. 'Come on and dance. Look,' as she had made no move, 'forget Cameron, will you? He's out of your league, your world, your reach, whatever you like to call it. It's your holiday, isn't it, the only one you'll get this year?'

'I'm spending another week at home with my parents.'

'So make the most of this place while you're here. Come on.' He had held out his hand.

'I don't trust you.'

'Trust me not to what? Make love to you? I will if you like, with the greatest pleasure.'

'No! No man after Zander's going to——' She stopped, aghast at what she might have given away. It seemed the man was not slow to grasp the unspoken, since he smiled unpleasantly.

'So it got that far, did it?'

Lisa made as if to go, but he caught her arm. 'Come on, one dance won't kill you. And I can't do a thing to you on the dance floor, especially with your friends here.'

A gesture with her hands had showed capitulation and a degree of resignation where the entire circumstances were concerned. This man's company was something she would not willingly have chosen, but dancing with him could surely do no harm. So she had accepted him as a partner.

Each evening was a repetition of the last. He made no effort to close the gap between them, stepped over no limits, respected her barriers. Now and then he had joined her as she had sunbathed on the beach. They had talked impersonally, swum separately and parted casually.

When they finally left the island that morning, Reg Beckley had already left for work. Their acquaintance had been too impersonal for them even to say goodbye to each other.

Myra and Phil had hugged her before going on their way. They were returning to their home, which was a room in Myra's parents' house. One day, Lisa had heard Phil say, we'll have enough money saved up for a place of our own.

Turning the key to let herself into her first-floor flat, Lisa almost stumbled over the pile of mail and free newspapers. Dropping her suitcases, she pushed aside the newspapers, annoyed that they had been delivered even when she was away, and seized on the mail.

There were cards from friends on holiday, mail order advertising, leaflets, bills and, at the bottom of the pile, a large, stiffened envelope. The address had been handwritten and there was a London postmark. It was the one she had been looking for, hoping for and almost despairing of receiving.

Putting everything else aside, she went into the living-room, tearing open the flap as she went. In a photographic envelope, there were about a dozen colour pictures. In vain she looked for a letter, an address, or even a brief message.

All she found was a piece of paper torn from a notebook. It bore the words, To Lisa, from Z. She stared at the words for a long time. He had not even given her his signature to hide away and keep in a secret place.

The photographs were so evocative of the time and the place, she wanted to cry. He had even included the picture taken by Reg Beckley, when they were wrapped in each other's arms.

With shaking hands, she replaced them in the envelope. Staring into the distance, she saw, not the pleasantly decorated room, nor the worn but comfort-

able chairs, but a beach of golden sand, a blue sea
stretching to a clear horizon, a tall man standing beside
her, stretching out his arm and removing her sun-
glasses, the better to see her eyes, he had said, which
were bluer than the sea.

Next day, Lisa spent washing and drying clothes and
generally preparing herself mentally for a return to
work. Her spirits were low and she told herself it was
the 'Monday morning feeling' reaching backwards into
the weekend.

The welcome she received from her office colleagues
was warm, if a little distracted. The manager of
Personnel had taken his vacation a week early, leaving
his deputy with twice her normal work-load.

'Sorry to have to ask you the very day you come
back,' Miss Harris, the deputy manager, apologised,
'but there's such a pile of mail, I was wondering if you
could manage some overtime this evening?'

Since she had little else to do, Lisa agreed, not really
sorry to have something with which to occupy her
restless mind. Having eaten a light evening meal in the
staff restaurant on the top floor of the ten-storey
building, she stepped out of the lift and walked towards
her own office.

Wondering how long it would take her to get through
the letters that awaited her attention, she happened to
glance along the corridor. In the near distance was a
man about to enter a room. He wore a grey suit and a
deep blue tie. He was tall, his hair was dark ... *and he
was clean-shaven*.

He must have become aware of being stared at, since
his gaze was drawn towards her. Lisa's hand went to
her mouth, then her throat. The corridor seemed to
sway, first one side, then the other. Opening her eyes
again, she saw he was standing a few paces away.

Under her hand, her cheek felt icy. She knew now
where she had seen that unbearded face before. Here, in
one of the Thistle International's annual reports. So he
was one of the company's top executives. Yet he had
told her so many lies!

'Have you recovered from the surprise?' His voice

was cold, his mouth hard, the expression in his eyes withdrawn.

'Yes, thank you.' It was impossible to prevent herself from studying his face, searching, searching for the warmth that had gone, seemingly for ever.

'I kept my promise.' He rubbed his chin. He spoke tonelessly. 'I warned you that you'd regret the consequences.'

'What you do hardly concerns me, does it?' How am I managing, she wondered, to sound so indifferent.

'So you know I have a fiancée.' Lisa nodded. 'Who told you?'

'Reg Beckley.'

The lips, so full and sensual now she could see them clearly, became a thin line. He lifted his wrist, which had retained its tan, and consulted his watch. 'What are you doing here?'

'I work here.'

Irritation pleated his brow. 'I'm aware of that. At this late hour, I mean.'

'I'm working overtime at the request of the deputy manager. The manager himself is on holiday.' Zander nodded, there was a heart-twisting pause, then he started to turn away. 'Thank you for the photographs,' she said softly. 'I didn't expect them, because I didn't give you my address.'

He answered with ego-shattering indifference, 'I asked my secretary to look it up in the files.' His manner did not alter as he added, 'Another promise kept.'

Lisa hesitated, but because she felt as if there was an open wound inside her, she made herself ask, 'Do you keep *all* your promises?'

They were both aware that it was a deeply serious question.

'Every single one,' he replied, 'without exception.'

Lisa could not nod for the pain. Opening the office door, she went in, walked unsteadily to her chair and dropped into it. Resting her elbows on the desk, she held her face. So many untruths he'd told her, so many evasions . . . So much sweet-talk, so many falsely happy hours, so much selfish lovemaking!

All right, so she had known their acquaintance would end in parting, but not this way, with this terrible, unbridgeable chasm yawning between them.

'Feeling ill, dear?' asked Miss Harris, emerging from her office.

Lisa mumbled that she had a headache.

'Why didn't you tell me? I'd never have expected you to stay late. You'd better go.'

Lisa shook her head furiously. Go home and face that emptiness? Quickly she seized a sheet of headed paper and began to type. The telephone in Miss Harris's office rang. Lisa typed on. Miss Harris returned.

'A message from Mr Cameron's secretary. Seems he's been here for a day or two, up from the country where he lives and works. She said Mr Cameron saw you and thought you looked ill. He instructed me to tell you to go home.'

'There's no need for me to go home, Miss Harris.'

The grey-haired, kindly woman must have picked up the curious note of appeal. 'I'd have thought you'd jump at the chance! Anyway, you'll have to go, dear, since the order came from Mr Alexander himself.'

Lisa frowned. 'Mr Alexander?'

'Yes, we call him that to distinguish him from his father, Mr Alasdair Cameron. He's in charge of the Scottish-based office near Edinburgh. Mr Alasdair Cameron's the president of the company. It's said that when Mr Alexander Cameron's father retires, he will take over.' Miss Harris seemed puzzled. 'You've worked here six months, dear—I thought you'd have known.'

Lisa smiled. 'When we secretaries talk among ourselves, we don't discuss the high and mighty men at the top.' She caught a touch of sarcasm in her own voice.

Miss Harris must have put it down to the headache, since she did not comment. Waiting while Lisa put the cover on her typewriter, she watched the movement, saying, 'I heard you talking outside just now. I thought I recognised Mr Alexander's voice, too.'

The woman was no fool and Lisa knew she would have to be truthful. 'It's true,' she admitted, 'that I was speaking to Mr Cameron.'

Miss Harris waited hopefully. Realising that no further explanation was forthcoming, she commented lightly, 'I didn't know you knew him, dear.'

'I don't really.' Lisa pulled on a lightweight jacket and picked up her bag. Well, she thought, it's true I don't know him—in the most fundamental sense of the word. And never will, her inner voice reminded her bleakly.

After a second night of tossing and turning, Lisa rose early and took a shower. It freshened her, but her rise in spirits gave way to anxiety as she entered the towering office block which formed Thistle International's head office.

Taking the stairs to the fourth floor instead of the lift, an action which she hoped would minimise her chances of meeting Zander Cameron, she found her eyes seeking round every corner for that commanding, dark-haired figure.

Having hurried, she reached her office earlier than the others. When Myra came in, they greeted each other like long-lost friends.

'I heard,' said Myra, 'that Mr A. Cameron, son of Mr A. Cameron, was in London for a few days from his place in Oxfordshire. I'd love to see him. They say he's really something!'

Miss Harris had not yet arrived, which left Lisa free to speak openly. 'How did you know,' she asked Myra, 'about Mr A. and Mr A.?'

Myra seized a sheet of company paper. 'Haven't you ever looked at the directors' names at the bottom?' She pointed. 'Mr A., Mr A., Mr H.——'

'Who's Mr H.?'

'Hamish Cameron, Mr Alexander Cameron's brother and Mr Alasdair Cameron's younger son. There's loads of other names. You can read them for yourself.'

'Is Hamish a working director, like the others?'

Myra shrugged, sitting on the corner of Lisa's desk. 'I

think he's supposed to be. They say there's usually a black sheep in a family. I'm told by my immediate boss that in the Cameron family, he's the one. He hasn't been seen around the place for a year or so now. No one seems to know where he is.'

The office clock told whoever looked at it that time did not stand still. Lisa calculated that it wouldn't be long before Miss Harris arrived to start her day's work.

'Myra, there's something you should know. No, not that,' Lisa smiled as Myra anxiously inspected her anatomy, 'but—well, you're not going to believe this. Remember Zander?'

'He's not the kind of man anyone could easily forget, is he? You mean you've heard from him?'

'More than that. I've seen him, and talked to him. Here, Myra, here. In this building.' Her voice dropped as if she hadn't really taken it in herself. 'He's the second Mr A. Cameron.'

'Alexander? How can he be? He was Zander, not——' The truth hit her. 'Short for Alexander?' Her eyes were as wide open as they ever could be.

'Minus beard, Myra,' Lisa added. 'He looks a different man. He warned me if he ever shaved his beard off, I wouldn't like the man I saw. He was right— I don't like that man.'

'But you still—dare I say it?—love him?'

Lisa was shaking her head. 'It was infatuation.' It was not, her heart contradicted, it was love. What's more, she thought sadly, it still is.

'Poor you,' Myra commiserated. 'And he's engaged, too.' She went to the door. 'You'll have to look for someone else. That's the best way to get over a man— find another.'

Lisa laughed at such worldly wisdom from her friend, who had had the same boy-friend since she was seventeen and who, at twenty-two, had married him. Myra opened the door, only to discover Miss Harris about to enter. 'See you around,' said Myra, wishing Miss Harris good morning on her way out.

'I've just met Shirley, Mr Cameron's secretary,' Miss Harris announced, smoothing her hair. 'They need

extra secretarial help. Shirley asked if I could spare you,
and of course I had to say yes. When the boss asks . . .'
She spread her hands, palms upwards, in a who-could-
argue-with-him action. 'He's going to let me have two
fresh secretaries in exchange for you.'

Lisa was puzzled. 'Was it really Mr Cameron who
asked, or was it Shirley who had the bright idea?'

'Definitely Mr Cameron,' replied Miss Harris, going
into her office.

Lisa had her own ideas on the subject. After their
close acquaintance—or was it called relationship
nowadays?—on the island of Lanzarote, she was sure
Zander would not want her brought into such close
contact with him.

Miss Harris returned, having disposed of her bag
and other belongings. 'The point is,' she informed
Lisa, 'Shirley's husband has got himself a job in the
north of England, which means she'll have to leave
and go with him. Mr Cameron wants you trained to
take her place.'

Lisa felt her cheeks grow warm and hoped Miss
Harris would not notice. 'Why me?' she asked,
genuinely puzzled.

'That's just what Shirley and I were saying, dear. In
fact, Shirley was under the impression, as I was, that
Mr Cameron didn't know of your existence.'

'Take a seat, Miss Maynard,' Zander Cameron's
secretary invited. 'Mr Cameron's on the phone. I'll buzz
him as soon as he's finished and tell him you're here.'
The attractive young woman at the desk smiled. 'Were
you surprised to hear about this changeover?'

Lisa laughed. 'It hasn't happened yet.'

The secretary smiled knowingly. 'It will. What Mr
Cameron says goes in this company. By the way, I'm
Shirley. Everyone calls me that.'

'I'm Lisa.' Shirley nodded as if she already knew. She
looked at the switchboard. 'Looks like he's finished on
the phone.' She lifted up the internal calls receiver. 'Mr
Cameron, Miss Maynard is here.

'He says you can go in. Don't look so nervous,'

Shirley encouraged, making Lisa smile. 'He won't eat you or even bite.'

I know that, she thought. He sets a trap instead, baits it with beautiful lies, then squeezes the life out of your heart when the trap snaps shut and snares you.

As she entered, he lifted himself from his chair behind the desk. Lisa wondered whether he showed such politeness to his secretary each time she walked in. Their eyes met and it was she who averted her eyes first. Just seeing him where he really belonged, a distinguished member of an international concern, filled her with despair.

Strange, she thought, how when he wore a beard, she had wanted it off so that she could see—and, as she thought, love—the man behind it. Now that beard had gone, the man she had come to know and love had gone, too.

'Lisa.' Something sprang to life inside her as she heard him speak her name so softly. If she had closed her eyes, she could have imagined them both back on that beach, making feverish love as the tide had started to cover them.

He motioned her to a chair. Gladly she occupied it. He was seated now and as their eyes met again, his were cool and without expression. His hands were clasped on a pile of papers, his gold watch gleamed against his sun-darkened skin. He had removed his jacket and his breadth of shoulder pushed at the shirt fabric.

He had been watching her all the time her gaze had wandered over him. He had been returning her stare, looking at her face, her bare arms, her neat blue dress. Just knowing his eyes were on her made her shiver, but she suppressed it.

'Well?' His question shot like a bullet across the deep silence.

It hit her somewhere in the region of her ribs. The pain beneath them was such that she reacted like a victim crying out. 'How could you?' she reproached.

Zander leaned back holding the chair arms. 'How could I what?'

'Make me think what I did—that you were a loner,

travelling from place to place, with no ties, no settled home.'

'If you deduced all that from what I said, I can't be blamed.'

Her eyes defied him. 'It was what you didn't say . . .'

He leaned forward again. 'I'm saying something now. I want you as my secretary. You'll be trained by Shirley before she goes. Your salary will be increased, your status will take a jump up the scale.'

'I won't be your secretary!' Her voice was intense. 'I'm telling you I don't want the job—and the status can go jump in the lake. But thanks for the offer.'

His teeth came together, his fist clenched and lifted in the act of striking the desk. He took hold and the fist stilled, frozen in the air.

Slowly, it lowered to rest and relax on the desk top. 'If I told you you had a choice—acceptance or face dismissal, which would you choose?'

'Dismissal.'

It took two seconds for his frost-coated eyes to bring a chill to hers. 'Right. Dismissal, as from now. The money owed to you by the company will be sent on.'

Her face went white under her tan. 'You can't mean it?'

The telephone rang. Zander lifted the receiver and listened. 'Yes, put him through.'

Lisa made to rise, still unable to take it in, certain he was fooling. When he began talking to the caller and sorting through his papers for a certain document, she straightened. She managed to reach the door. Her hand shook as she moved the handle. Half-turning, she caught his look withdrawing. He had been watching her progress across the room.

It meant nothing. Only one thing mattered. He had not called her back.

After her meal that evening, Lisa phoned Myra, who refused to believe a single word.

'Mr Cameron doesn't do things like that—especially to you. I mean, after what happened on holiday——'

'Nothing happened on holiday, Myra, not really.'

'Okay, I accept that. But why, oh, why did you turn down that absolute gift of a job? You must be mad, Lisa! I don't want to upset you, but you are my friend, and if friends can't be frank with each other, who can?'

'I know I'm mad. But I just couldn't take it. Working for him and with him every day and all day, don't you understand what I mean?'

'All I can say is that you're mad twice over. One, for refusing his job. Two, for falling for him so hard. I mean, doesn't the fact that he's engaged make you see sense?'

'You mean, make me realise he's way beyond my reach?' Myra was trying her best to help, so she agreed, 'You're probably right. If I say over and over again to myself, "He's engaged," maybe I'll get to believing it. Anyway,' the realisation returning hit her hard, 'it doesn't matter any more, does it? I'll never see him again.'

'That's true. But what a pity he had to go and sack you. Will he give you a good reference, do you think?'

'Let's hope any request for one doesn't reach that high in the company hierarchy. I'll give the personnel manager's name each time. After all,' she added, before she rang off, 'he was my immediate boss.'

Lisa flung into a chair and closed her eyes. Pictures floated before them, highly-coloured, flooded with sunlight, golden beaches and white houses and cacti as tall as trees. It was strange how she could see herself in Zander's arms, dancing, standing on the hotel's highest balcony, or in the cave's darkness, gazing into the deep, coin-starred pool, as if she were watching scenes from a film, and not taking part.

Raking in a drawer for the photographs which Zander had taken, she gazed at each one for a long time. In the end, she gave up pretending that it was not she who was clasped in Zander's arms, or who gazed at him so fondly, or who smiled with such windblown, abandoned happiness at the man who was taking the shot.

It was easier, she discovered, to accept that the man was not Alexander Cameron. That laughing, bearded, relaxed figure was a different person from the fast-thinking, clean-shaven, icy-eyed sniper who had shot her down that morning.

I'll never see him again. The words she had spoken to Myra on the phone started to spin in her brain, forming a wheel and then a circle until she had to cover her eyes to obliterate them.

The outside bell rang. As she rose automatically to answer, the photographs scattered like a house of cards. The building shook around her—or was it she who was shaking the building?—when she saw the man who stood outside.

'I'd have worn a false beard if I'd thought it would have made you smile.'

'Smile,' he had said, and Lisa could have cried as she remembered that 'stamp album' of her smiles he had promised he would keep.

'There are no smiles left inside me since before my vacation ended,' she shot back.

Zander did not even rock on his feet. Under the pull of her hand, the door opened wider, and she cursed her automatic reflexes for letting him in.

'What did you do,' he indicated the scattered photographs, 'vent your anger on them?'

'If I had,' she snapped, 'they would by now have been torn to shreds!' Bending, she retrieved a photograph, one she had taken of him, looked at it, looked at him, started to throw it in the waste bin, but changed her mind. The photograph she pressed to her heart, the man she made a target for mental daggers.

He smiled as if he could read her thoughts, 'Decided to chuck away the man, instead?'

'You're so right,' she hurled at him. 'This man,' she held out the picture, 'was human and lovable. He was a fantasy man. The reality,' she motioned towards him with her hand, 'is a nightmare.'

'Thanks for that,' he came back dryly, looking round for an armchair and dropping into one. 'I should have bought that false beard, after all. Then I could have walked right back into your dreams.'

'It was a false beard you wore on the island. It was as

unreal as the personality you assumed.' Lisa was walking about, unable to rest. 'You told me so many lies, that's what I can't forgive you for.'

He was so still she turned to look at him. It was, she decided, a foolish move on her part. It enabled her to see his long legs stretched out as if he belonged, the worn slacks that hugged his thighs, the leanness above the belted waist. His shirt was partly opened, showing a triangle of deep tan.

His brown eyes were smiling at her scrutiny, their lazy luminescence slanted at her with the male assessment which had made her heart trip the first time she had seen him. Her body, her flesh was remembering the touch of him, making her want to run into this man's arms. *This* man—not that tyrant behind the office desk.

It was necessary to make her feminine instincts see reason, and hear it, too. Turning on him, she accused, 'You lied in so many ways. By inference, telling me the world was your oyster. By evasion, pretending you were only on nodding terms with the name Thistle International, when all the time you were one of its top executives.'

He folded his arms, lowered his lids and waited, as if he were prepared to let her talk the censure out of her system. As she talked, she began to convince herself, and her instincts, that she hated the man who had fired her so pitilessly that day, this man who occupied a chair in her apartment into which he had walked uninvited.

Looking at the photograph which she still held, she said, 'You told me you didn't have a wife, but you omitted to tell me that you had a fiancée. What was that but evasion?'

His lips stayed closed, his eyes narrowed and watchful.

Lisa sat at last, needing support. 'That—that nonsense about liking my smile.' The anger in her voice had given way to sadness. 'That was a lie, too.' She raised her eyes to challenge his. 'You only paid me all those compliments to get what you wanted.'

'You think that?' Zander hauled himself out of the

chair and caught her arm, pulling her up to join him.
His hand slipped under the thickness of her rich brown
hair, easing her head forward and upward, the better to
take his kiss.

She twisted and turned her head. 'I won't let you kiss
me! You're an engaged man, you've no right to be
making love to anyone but your fiancée!'

His fingers tightened on the back of her head, forcing
it to be still. He appeared not to have heard her, so
intent was he on getting his own way. His lips made a
takeover bid for hers and she let them go without a
fight.

Closing her eyes, she could forget the mundane
surroundings of her apartment, replacing it with the
luxury of a hotel room outside which was the sound,
not of the constant flow of traffic, but the swish and
wash of breaking waves.

It was easier, too, to imagine that the man whose
arms held her was the lean, muscled man in the
photograph. So when her mouth started returning his
kisses, accepting them and giving them back with an
almost abandoned eagerness, she did not reproach it.

His hands were massaging the back of her neck, then
reaching to rediscover the inviting curves of her, sliding
inside to fondle her breast. His enticing touch brought
her to the edge of forgetfulness of the time and the
place, transporting her from reality to a higher plain—
of dreams, and love's fulfilment.

Descending to ground-level living, her mind stumbled.
What was she doing in this man's arms, allowing him to
change her back into the bright-eyed, infatuated girl
with whom he had amused himself on that island?
Shaking off the weakness that had turned her limbs to
water, quenching the fire he had started in her loins, she
pulled away from him.

'Well?' he asked, pulling her back against him. His
voice was husky, his brown eyes languorous and sexy. It
was necessary to steel her mind and every part of her
against the magnetic pull of him. 'Do you remember
now if my compliments were merely a preliminary to
getting "what I wanted"?'

Lisa was silent, fighting the urge to trace his lips, the impact from which hers were still throbbing.

Zander shook her a little. 'Think back to the night we spent together.' She turned her face away, but he turned it towards him again. 'I exercised self-control, did I not? You almost pleaded with me to go on?'

Lisa jerked but he gripped her arms, forcing up her face. He would not even allow her to hide her humiliation.

'And we talked about the possibility of a child?'

'Don't keep reminding me!' she cried out in pain.

He had no mercy. 'I said you'd remember me as the man who held back of his own accord, without your having to impose the embargo.'

'Yes, yes. And you quoted Robert Burns. I agree, I agree. Now let me go.'

His grip on her held, and she knew that, in the morning, she would find bruises. 'And,' his voice had softened, 'I called you "my bonnie dearie".'

'I know you did, quoting Burns again. But it all meant nothing, did it? Your endearments were meaningless. And you only stopped yourself from going all the way because you had a fiancée.'

He let her go, pushing her away. His fine eyes had hardened, his chin jutted, his hands thrust into his pocket.

A small tremor shook Lisa's hand as she used it to smooth her hair which he had ruffled, to button her dress which he had begun to unfasten.

'In Lanzarote,' she declared, fighting his eyes with hers, 'you used me, despite the self-control you boasted about. You were missing your fiancée, so you used your bait to coax me——'

He frowned coldly. 'My bait?'

'Your eyes, there was a look in them . . . They said "come".'

His smile was coloured by cyncisim. 'So, at their invitation, you came, just like that.' He snapped his fingers. 'You didn't have to, did you? If you hadn't wanted to be hooked by my bait, you could have told me with those blue eyes to get lost.'

'And,' she tried to match his cynicism with sarcasm, 'you would have "got lost", of course!'

His slightly lustful gaze travelled over her. 'That's a difficult one. You've got one hell of a lot going for you.'

'Thank you kindly. My ex-boy-friend didn't seem to think so.' Feeling weary of the cut and thrust of their unending battle—he held the sharper sword—Lisa sought her seat. 'If—if I did respond to your invitation——'

'You did.'

'——it was because I was lonely. Being odd one out to a newly-married couple is no fun, especially when you're on holiday.' He made a disbelieving sound and her head jerked up. She was about to twist the truth. 'It was nothing to do with your "irresistible" charms, as you seem to think. You were quite unscrupulous,' she added. 'Like this morning, when you fired me.'

'Oh, no,' he walked nearer, looking down at her, 'you don't lay that little episode on my doorstep. You fired yourself.'

The truth of the statement could not be disputed. Rising to her feet, she looked at him, holding down the treacherous need to be enveloped by those arms.

'I came to withdraw my dismissal notice, but,' he declared, going towards the door, 'since you've called me unscrupulous, I'll live up to that label. Let the dismissal stand.'

'Zander!'

It was like a yelp from a wounded animal. He was almost through the door. Her feet took her flying after him. Her hand grabbed his arm, but he jerked it free. 'What do you want?' he grated.

He was forcing her to plead! 'My job back. Give me my job back.'

He was in the room again. 'As my secretary?'

'Yes, yes. Please!' Anything to be near him again . . .

There was the mystery of a darkened cavern in his gaze, then it was gone.

'First thing tomorrow, go to Shirley's office. In a week's time it will be yours.'

He had gone before she could thank him.

CHAPTER SEVEN

THAT week was a long one, but Lisa learned a great deal. She learned that Mr Cameron demanded as much dedication from his secretary in her work as he gave to it. He liked his secretary to be quick and precise and accurate. Whenever there was a particularly heavy work load, he expected her to stay late with him and carry on working until the load had disappeared.

Mr Cameron was often away, too, either in Scotland seeing his father on company business or abroad for the same reason. In Mr Cameron's absence, Shirley explained, pressures increased rather than lessened. Telephone enquiries had to be dealt with without Mr Cameron's guidance. Letters needed to be answered, even if they were only fill-ins until the boss returned.

'It's a well-paid job,' Shirley stated, 'but you're almost worked off your feet for the money.' She smiled. 'Sure you can take it?' It was the last day of the week and it was a question that Lisa knew had to be asked.

'I can take everything Mr Cameron cares to give,' Lisa replied, sounding far more confident than she felt.

'I'm glad to hear it, Miss Maynard.' The deep, amused voice came from the interconnecting doorway. He smiled at the colour he had produced in her cheeks. 'Shirley, what is your honest opinion of my secretary-to-be's ability?'

Shirley smiled at Lisa. 'You don't mind if I'm brutally frank, do you?'

Lisa shook her head, her heart sinking. From having refused the position at the start, she had passed to wanting it very much indeed. Not only would she be near to Zander for many hours of the day—she did not pause to consider if this would be fair to her own wellbeing in view of her feelings for the man—she was determined to meet the challenge the job contained.

'Well,' Shirley was saying, 'I think she'll do you proud.'

Lisa smiled her gratitude at Shirley, then turned to dare with her eyes the man to whom the statement had been made. The daring changed to a questioning at the flash of warmth she caught in his returning gaze. It was gone before she could be certain and before it could be intercepted by the young woman who watched them both.

Lisa's dread that Shirley might have sensed the hidden link between them was dispelled when she exclaimed, 'Thank goodness I haven't trodden on anybody's toes!' To Lisa, she said, 'I meant it, I didn't intend to flatter.'

Zander laughed and Lisa revelled in the sound. She had not heard it since that last night they had spent together at the holiday hotel. 'I'm well aware you speak your mind, Shirley. I know from experience that Lisa does, too, so your outspokenness has been a good training ground for my new secretary's.'

Lisa darted a look at Shirley, wondering if it had occurred to her to wonder at Mr Cameron's apparently extensive knowledge of the character of the girl he was supposed only to have met less than a week ago.

Shirley did look puzzled, but the moment passed. As if to wipe the slate clean on the subject, the telephone rang on cue. Shirley reached to answer it, stopped and asked Lisa, with raised eyebrows, if she would do so instead.

Not only was Shirley supervising her, but Zander Cameron was watching. This is where it all begins, Lisa thought tensely, and took the call. As she listened and answered, having fortunately picked up this necessary piece of information during the week, her tension left her and she dealt easily with the query.

When the call ended, Shirley clapped her hands together, saying, 'I knew you'd handle the job without any trouble. Mr Cameron, you've picked a winner here.'

The quick glint in his eyes as they rested momentarily on her told her that his thoughts had darted back in time. Hers were not slow to follow.

'I can only do my best,' she declared at last, at which

Zander nodded, then appeared to dismiss the subject from his mind.

Lisa travelled home that Friday evening feeling that the weekend which stretched ahead would be a long one. She had called Myra on the internal telephone and told her the news. Myra had showered her with congratulations. Letting herself into her apartment, she told herself how crazy she was to have allowed herself to get to the stage, this early in her new job, when she considered every moment spent away from Zander Cameron to be a waste of time.

He's an engaged man, she told her headstrong thoughts. Preparing her meal after washing and changing into a cotton dress, she came to the inescapable conclusion that until his fiancée materialised, she would not be able to bring herself to acknowledge the girl's existence.

Shirley had not mentioned the possibility, probably through loyalty to her employer, but Lisa, seating herself at the breakfast bar with her cottage cheese salad, was certain the woman must often have appeared in the secretary's office, demanding immediate access to her husband-to-be. The idea that Zander could be some other woman's husband-to-be caused Lisa to put down her fork and close her eyes until the pain had gone.

The weekend passed just as slowly, with only a phone call from Myra to ask her whether she was sure she would like her new job. 'I've had a good report from Shirley, who seems to think I shall manage it without any trouble.'

'How do you feel about yourself?' Myra probed.

Lisa paused to consider. 'I'm in a fighting mood,' she asserted. 'I'll be verbally battered into submission by no one, least of all, Mr A. Cameron.'

Myra laughed. 'Good for you! I hope you'll stand up to him even in his foulest mood, and according to my boss, Mr A. really does have them.'

'Myra,' Lisa interposed, with a surge of anxiety, 'you haven't told anyone, have you? I mean about Zander and myself in Lanzarote?'

'As if I would, Lisa. I'm your best friend, aren't I? Oh, and Phil sends his love.'

'Thanks. Myra, before you go—have you ever seen Zander's fiancée? No? Has anyone in this place, ever?'

'Not that I know of. But she's reputed to be cool, self-centred and possessive. Her name's Corinna Allen, if you'd like to know.'

Lisa frowned. 'The name's vaguely familiar.'

'Well, if it's any help, she used to be a top model. Given it up now, at her fiancé's insistence, or so they say.'

'Which must surely mean she's beautiful?'

'Could be, dear. Look, Lisa, you must stop fretting about the man. He's not for you. There are so many pointers that way. Surely you can see them?'

'I guess I would, if I weren't so stupidly blind. You know what they say about love.'

'*Love?* That's something you mustn't do, Lisa. After knowing him for such a short time, how can you possibly know enough about him to love him? For heaven's sake!'

'It happens,' Lisa answered sadly, 'it happens.' She sighed. 'See you and Phil some time. 'Bye!'

Monday morning began with a headlong plunge into work. A week, Lisa thought, panic in her movements, was not nearly long enough in which to take in every possible aspect of the job.

Her employer's standards were of the highest. He might allow one mistake, but more than that would, she was sure, cause him such annoyance that a dismissal as swift and deadly as the one she herself had instigated would surely be a certainty. And this time there would be no magnanimous withdrawal.

Such thoughts caused her panic to intensify to such a pitch that she discovered the moistness of her hands was leaving telltale marks on the letters she was opening for him.

Hurriedly she sought a handkerchief and rubbed at her hands. At that moment the cause of her panic came in, through the communicating door. He looked at the action with a frown, then came across to her. Stuffing her handkerchief away, she stared at him guiltily.

He reached out and took a hand, wrapping his own round it. He had held her hand many times in that time they had had of getting to know each other, but then it had been for frivolous, happy reasons. This was a testing action, and it was with a growing anxiety that she awaited his verdict.

'Fear, Miss Maynard?' His eyes were excluded from his fleeting smile. 'Of what? The job, your ability to do it, or of me?'

'All three, Mr Cameron.' Her words came out cracked and dry.

This time his eyes smiled without his mouth. 'The first two only you can come to terms with. Maybe, the third,' he bent down and his mouth brushed hers, once, twice, 'might be overcome by that?'

Lisa shook her head, trying to quell the shiver of pleasure his action created. 'I know all about those, Mr Cameron. They went with the man I knew on the island. He was a great guy, Mr Cameron.' Her voice wavered a fraction. 'I—I could have got to like him a lot.' Her hand was released and dropped to her side. 'This man and you are as different as summer and winter.'

'Meaning,' the brown eyes grew hard, 'that this man,' he pointed to his own chest, 'is winter.'

'Yes, Mr Cameron. So those kisses don't work any more, Mr Cameron.'

'For heaven's sake stop calling me Mr Cameron!' The words ground through his teeth.

'But I'm your secretary, Mr Cameron.' She took a steadying breath at his expression. 'Sorry—sir.'

'For heaven's sake, that's worse! Stick to——'

'Yes, Mr Cameron.' Her eyes were laughing, she could not help it. Her lips widened into the first real smile she had managed for many days.

He smiled at her smile and reached out, gripping the bare flesh of her upper arm to pull her to him. The phone rang. He released her and made for his office. 'For heaven's sake, shut that thing up!'

Reaching out, Lisa obeyed. Five minutes later she replaced the receiver. She felt pleased with herself for

having dealt successfully with her first enquiry entirely
unaided.

It was next morning that her world turned upside down.
Finding that her employer was surprisingly late in
arriving, she racked her brains to remember whether he
had given her any explanation that might have escaped
her memory.

Then she searched around on her desk for a mislaid
memo. There was nothing. The post had been opened
and left neatly in a pile awaiting his attention. There
had been one or two phone calls from business
acquaintances asking to speak to him.

It was mid-morning and her coffee cup stood empty
on a side table. He still had not arrived. Hesitating as to
whether to contact one of the other directors, asking
them if they knew the reason for Zander's absence, a
piece of information given to her by Shirley drifted
back into her mind.

'His main place of working,' Shirley had told her,
'isn't here in London. He lives and works in Churwood,
a small town in north Oxfordshire.'

'I knew the company had offices there,' Lisa
remembered replying.

'Not exactly office, as such,' Shirley had told her. 'It's
a house, a large one. And old, but fully modernised.
You known, en suite bathrooms and showers. It's all
tastefully decorated, too. It's good to work in such an
atmosphere.'

'It sounds as though you've been there,' Lisa had
commented.

'A number of times, and for a few weeks at a time.
When I married Stan, though, he objected to my
staying over, so I've worked from here ever since, while
Mr Cameron did the commuting.'

Lisa remembered Shirley's final words on the subject.
'Mr Cameron will probably want you to transfer there,
though. Seems he doesn't like leaving his fiancée for too
long.'

Lisa rolled a pencil back and forward. Strange, she
reflected, how that painful piece of information had

been suppressed by her subconscious mind. At the time, it had been like a knife being thrust under her ribs.

When the telephone rang, she knew instinctively the identity of the caller.

'Lisa?' The tone was abrupt, strictly boss to secretary.

Assuming her correct role immediately, she answered accordingly.

'I want you to collect all the current files and documents, the post and anything else relevant to the particular contract we're dealing with. Right?'

'Yes, Mr Cameron.' Her heart rate was revving up like a racing car testing its engine. Had she guessed what was coming now?

'I also want you to return to your apartment, collect some clothes and your personal belongings—enough for two or three weeks—and come across to Churwood.'

After a stunned pause, she asked, 'Just like that, Mr Cameron?'

'Just like that, Miss Maynard.' There was no mockery there, just a curtness which chilled. 'A car will call for you at two o'clock,' he continued, 'before which I'll expect you to have had some lunch. Have you got that?'

'Every word, Mr Cameron,' she answered, hoping he had received her silent message that she had recovered her balance and was taking everything in her stride.

Only when she put down the telephone did she allow herself to acknowledge that she still had not adjusted to the idea of the approaching change in her life-pattern.

Worst of all was the thought that before many hours had passed, she would be meeting the fiancée of the man she had grown to love, the fiancée who, according to Shirley, he didn't like leaving for long.

The journey was tiring, but the car offered every comfort. The company driver was not, Lisa was glad to discover, a talkative man.

In boxes, she had packed every file and folder she considered her employer might need. In her suitcase she had placed clothes for warm days, for cool days, for walks in the country and even a long dress, just in case Mr Alexander Cameron, top executive, took it into his head to give a party.

Lisa rested her head against the breathing upholstery and wondered if she would ever feel in a party mood again. For most of her waking hours, and many of her nights, she tried her best to knit together the man she had known while on holiday with the man for whom she now worked.

Where had he gone, that carefree, relaxed, rather sensual individual who had kissed her and made her laugh, danced with her and made exquisite love? Zander had said he loved her smile so much he wanted to 'catch' it. He had said things to make her laugh, just to hear the sound. Where had he gone?

'Nearly there, miss,' the driver announced over his shoulder. 'Up this long drive, then we'll be at the house. It's a lovely house, isn't it, miss? Been here before, have you?'

'This is my first time,' Lisa answered. 'It certainly is impressive.'

The words, she felt as soon as she had spoken, were an understatement. The house was beautiful, with its numerous windows, white walls and green-slated roof. There was a flight of stone steps leading to the arched portico around the recessed, glass-paned front entrance door.

'What a pity,' she commented, as the car came to a stop on the gravelled, semi-circular drive outside the residence, 'it's not a real home.'

The driver got out, opening her door. 'It's as much a home as anyone else's, miss,' he defended. 'Mr Cameron's fiancée sees to that.'

'You mean—she lives here?'

He gave Lisa a darting look. 'Where else could she live, miss, in the circumstances?'

What circumstances? Lisa longed to ask, but the man plainly felt he had said enough. 'I'll show you the way,' he offered, indicating that she should climb the flight of stone steps.

Before he could raise the knocker, the door was

opened by a small-built, smiling woman. 'Have you brought us a new face, Edgar?' she said, pulling the door wider.

'Milly's my wife, miss,' the driver called Edgar explained. 'She's Mr Cameron's housekeeper. She'll look after you. I'll get the things from the car.'

As Lisa stepped inside, the hall widened out, seeming to take on enormous proportions. The carpet was dark-patterned, the furniture reproduction antique. Doors as solidly made as the house itself, led off in various directions. They did not so much invite, Lisa reasoned, as dared curious hands to turn their handles.

The staircase made a bold statement of its own existence, running wide and straight to a platform, then turning to continue on its grandly carved and carpeted way. The platform was not empty. A man with loosened tie and rolled shirt-sleeves, his hands in his pockets, stared down unsmilingly. His expression bore no welcome.

Only a weekend had passed since she had last seen him, yet it seemed like a year. He came slowly down the stairs, his eyes fixed on her.

'Three for dinner this evening, Mr Cameron?' the housekeeper enquired.

Zander nodded and she went away, saying over her shoulder, 'Tell me when you're ready, Miss Maynard, and I'll show you to your room.'

'Thank God you've come,' said Zander Cameron, and Lisa's heart skipped with joy, but it slowed to walking pace when he added, 'I'm up to my chin in work.'

His chin, she thought, which she could now see, square and resolute, his jaw, rigid and sweeping to tapering cheeks. Uncluttered lips which were full and sensual; arched, dark brows and hair now combed and shorter, but which she had seen windblown and unruly, wet from a shower or making love on damp sands . . .

Edgar deposited Lisa's cases to one side of the entrance hall, announcing that he would get the boxes.

'Do you want me to start work straight away?' Lisa

asked. 'I'm quite willing, except I'm thirsty?' It was a question, since she did not know her employer's routine in his home environment.

'I'm glad you're willing.' His voice came softly, his eyes played the game of reminiscing, taking on the veiled, sensual expression with which he had assessed her assets from the very first moment of their acquaintance. 'And I'm thirsty, too.' His gaze touched her well-shaped mouth and his meaning could not be mistaken.

Lisa coloured, a fact which seemed to amuse him. She looked around, hoping there was no door partly open, allowing his fiancée to hear their exchange. On the other hand, Lisa realised, the words had been innocent in themselves. It was the tension between them which had added the deeper meaning.

'The offices are upstairs,' he informed her, reverting to his usual detachment. 'I'll get Milly to bring us a tray.'

'That would be lovely,' Lisa declared, in a bright 'secretary' voice.

Zander, who had remained on the stairs, lifted a brow sardonically at her tone. Edgar returned with an armful of boxes. 'Usual place, sir?' he asked, and passed his employer on the stairs. 'There's more to come, sir,' Edgar remarked, chin on the top box to steady it.

'What have you done,' Zander enquired of Lisa, 'brought the whole contents of the London office with you?'

'Anything relevant, you told me on the phone,' here she realised how belligerent she must have sounded, and added jerkily, 'sir.'

Zander gave her a hard look, indicating with his head that she should follow him. At the top of the stairs, Edgar waited respectfully while they climbed up, then made his way speedily down, saying, 'One more journey should finish the job.'

Zander led Lisa along the carpeted landing and into a room which, she judged, must once have been a bedroom. Its shape was square, and heavy, fringed curtains hung on each side of the long windows. Angelic figures decorated the high ceiling, the walls were half wood-panelled, while paintings adorned the high expanse of wall above the panelling.

It was fashioned for living, breathing men and women to pass their nights in tasteful splendour. Yet the only furniture the room held was impersonal to the point of coldness.

Set at an angle was a desk which made no pretence at even a nodding acquaintance with the era in which the house was built. On the desk which Zander made for were at least four different coloured telephones. He picked up a receiver and ordered tea.

'You can drop the "sir".' The instruction came so abruptly, Lisa turned to face the speaker. 'If I hear you call me that again, I'll lower your salary. Do you understand?'

His eyes were as hard as the line of his lips. The air crackled as if with an electrical charge as their eyes met. She caught her breath at his look. There was no gentleness. It was as if he were making violent, savage love to her. The pain she felt in her limbs and her heart was as bruising as if he were squeezing the life out of her.

Abstractedly, she noticed that his fists were clenched as they rested on the desk top. His jaw was thrust forward as if a kind of anger filled his body.

Lisa felt her cheeks grow pale. 'What have I done that you should look at me like that?' she cried. 'When I called you "sir", it wasn't out of insolence, even if you chose to take it that way.' Approaching his desk, she begged, 'Please let's forget the past. Whatever happened between us is over. And nothing really did happen, did it? You had the sense to hold back. If you hadn't——'

'I must have been crazy to turn down your invitation.'

'Please, Zander,' she was pleading now, 'let it be. It's over, it's finished, isn't it?' It will never finish, she told her throbbing heart.

'The past never dies, Lisa. It tends, instead, to take on a greater significance as time passes.'

'We *must* forget. Otherwise how can I carry on working for you?' She walked to a smaller desk, walked

back. 'I don't understand you. You're engaged. Your
fiancée's beautiful, or so I'm told. Or——' it came out
of the blue, 'is she frigid? And did you have it in mind
to make me your——'

There was a knock and Edgar pushed at the door
with his foot. He was up to his chin again in boxes.
'Sorry I was so long, sir. Milly caught me for
something. She's bringing up your tray of tea and
biscuits in a couple of minutes.'

He took the boxes through a door and into an
adjoining room. Returning, he touched his cap and
went out. The interruption had happened at an
opportune moment, breaking the tension and infusing
the atmosphere with the formality of a boss-employee
relationship.

'I'll unfasten the boxes,' said Lisa, avoiding Zander's
eyes, and peered through the door to discover a smaller
room which was probably once a child's bedroom. It
contained a modern desk on which stood an electronic
typewriter. There were two or three other chairs of
varying sizes. Nearby stood a photocopier. This room,
she guessed, would be hers.

It was not long before Milly entered with the tray,
which she carried to a writing table near one of the two
windows. 'There you are, Miss Maynard. Now you can
quench your thirst. I'll pour the first two cups, shall I?'
She did so, adding, 'There are biscuits if you want
them. Try one. They're home-made.'

'By Milly herself,' Zander remarked. 'Refuse one at
your peril, Lisa.' His mood had undergone a lightning
change and she smiled, liking the feeling his use of her
first name created. It meant nothing, she reminded
herself at once. Didn't he call his ex-secretary Shirley?

Milly laughed on her way to the door. 'You always
appreciate my cooking, Mr Cameron.' She left them,
closing the door.

They met at the table and the nearness of him was
like thunder rumbling in Lisa's head. There was a storm
going on in her emotions, but she knew she would be
the only one to feel its ravaging effects.

He picked up a biscuit, holding it to her mouth.

'Open,' he commanded, and she laughed. He watched her eyes flash to brightness and smiled. 'Take a bite. Of biscuit, not my finger!'

Smiling, as she did as she was told, rolling her eyes expressively as she caught the taste. 'Mm, delicious,' she pronounced, taking it from him. He was drinking tea and watching her over the cup's rim. She seized her cup to hide her face, but she couldn't stop their eyes from meeting and holding.

They were plunging back in time and Lisa could almost see the blue sky, feel the sun's powerful rays tempered only by the winds roaring across from the African mainland. There was a spreading warmth inside her as if he was caressing her skin.

When the dream faded, she saw that he had withdrawn his gaze and was staring out of the window. She had been alone on Lanzarote. He had not followed her there.

His voice was distant as he said, 'I'd like to tackle as much as possible of the outstanding work. Will you be finished soon?'

'Yes, Mr Cameron,' she answered, and the words were toneless.

He glanced at her dispassionately, replaced his empty cup and returned to his desk. Moments later she joined him, showing him that morning's letters, standing back and awaiting his instructions.

We're back on course, she thought, in every way. Never again, she resolved, would she allow herself to stray from the well-marked path. Nor, she vowed, would she ever again allow her emotions or her memory to take her back into the past.

Lisa did not surface again until Edgar put his grey head round the office door.

'Dinner will be served, Mr Cameron, in forty minutes. Milly told me to tell you.'

Zander waved him away impatiently. It seemed Edgar was used to such brusque treatment, since he turned a bright smile to Lisa. She smiled back, an action which must have transformed her face so much, Edgar stared in admiration.

When the head had been withdrawn, she found Zander watching her. His mouth tightened in a cynical smile, but he did not speak. Ten minutes went by and Lisa looked down at her travel-worn skirt and jacket.

'Do you dress for dinner, Mr Cameron?' she ventured to ask.

His head came up from his reading. 'I dress for everything, Miss Maynard. Except, as you may remember,' his gaze zig-zagged from the top of her head to her sandalled feet, 'bed.'

Her cheeks coloured and she was furious with them for betraying her embarrassment. 'What I meant was, do you wear *long* dresses?'

'Do *I* wear long dresses?' he asked comically.

Lisa realised what she had said and her head went back in laughter. His look as he watched reminded her of the admiring expression on Edgar's face.

'Sorry, that's not what I really meant to say.'

'Thank God for that,' he quipped. 'For a moment you had me worried about myself!'

She grinned at him and he returned it in full measure, leaning back in his chair, becoming for a short moment the man called Zander she had grown to love.

He felt for his missing tie and leaned forward again, a frown having taken the place of the smile. 'Yes, you will be required to wear a long dress. I should have remembered to tell you. My fiancée insists on it.' He looked up again. 'Did you bring a long dress?'

'Luckily, yes. If not, I'd have had to wear a nightdress, wouldn't I, Mr Cameron?' She flicked him an impish smile.

'Have you actually gone back, Miss Maynard, to wearing nightdresses in bed?' He had scored against her, and he knew it.

Cursing the mounting, giveaway colour, Lisa rose. 'May I go and unpack now, please?' she asked, holding her bag.

'Do you know where your room is?' She shook her head. He levered himself from his chair. 'I'll take you there myself.'

Lisa walked beside him, climbing with him as he

mounted a curving flight of stairs. Opening a door, he stood back, inviting her to go in. 'It has its own bathroom. I hope you'll find it comfortable.'

Lisa entered, liking the room at once. Moving past her suitcases, which had been carried upstairs, she made for the doors which were opened on to a balcony. Her hands came together in delight at the view which greeted her.

At the end of the sloping lawn, in the distance, was a splash of blue, surrounded by a screen of bushes. Nearby was a wooden building and stretching away down a gentle hill was a patch of woodland.

Zander had come to join her. 'The pool's heated,' he explained, then pointed. 'That's a sun chalet which revolves to catch the sun. Just behind it is a tennis court. And the woods are there to lose yourself in when you can't take another directive from your boss.'

Lisa smiled up at him, turning towards the bedroom. There was a writing table, a chest of drawers. To one side of the bed was a long mirror, over the double bed two lights with switches. There was a dressing-table with drawers and another mirror, a stool pushed in.

The long curtains at the window and the balcony door were of the same patterned fabric as the bed covers. A round table stood beside the bed, the cloth which covered it also sharing the flowered, multi-coloured design. The carpeting was thick and a delicate blue. A glance into the bathroom told her it had everything a bathroom should have.

'It couldn't be nicer,' she told him with a happy smile. 'I think I'm going to enjoy working for you here, and living here.'

His eyes grew guarded for a fleeting moment, then his smile met hers.

'Feel free,' he said, 'to use all the facilities. Take a swim, bask in the sun chalet.'

'Get lost in the woods?'

With me. She was sure the words were on his lips, but a barrier seemed to spring up in his mind, keeping them in. His seriousness stole away her happy mood. There was something wrong. Had she been too familiar?

Couldn't he have told her? Didn't he understand how difficult it was for her to forget their closeness during that island holiday? It had seeped into her system, and it hadn't yet worked its way out. She wondered if it ever would.

Still he looked at her and it was as if he had taken a step backward in time. Did he hear the sound of waves breaking, the wind rushing by? He pulled her close and bent his head, finding the base of her throat and placing small kisses up to her ear.

There were words being whispered. What had he said? *Get lost in me, Lisa, lose yourself in me* ... He found her mouth at last, and it was as if they were back in that hotel bedroom. There was demand in every move of his head. He placed his lips at all angles across hers, then forced hers apart.

The kiss was as deep and searching as any he had given her, and Lisa was caught up in him again. The feel of his arms around her as they had been on the island took her back, too. Her arms locked round his neck and his hands began a recap of her bodily attractions, holding her breasts, moving down and down until he found her hips which he tugged against him, holding her there.

The heat of his desire was bringing her body back to life. His needs were clamouring at the door of hers, and she tried straining away from all contact. His strength was the greater and he easily overcame her struggles.

It was no use, she admitted to herself, none at all. Her hands overlapped on the back of his head, and she gave back every single kiss he was giving her. When he stopped, burying his face in her hair, she whispered,

'Zander, please stop!' He looked into her imploring eyes and she perceived that impatience and reason were at war inside him. She tried to soothe by saying, 'Robert Burns was wiser than we are, wasn't he? "Know prudent self-control is wisdom's root". You quoted that the day you left the island.'

'To hell with prudent self-control,' he said, his eyes hard with disappointed desire. He let her go, but with

irritation, as if she were to blame, as if she were the one
to have placed the embargo on his lovemaking.

'Your fiancée is waiting for you, isn't she?' Lisa
offered unhappily, turning from him to hide her pain.

After a few moments, he moved away. 'You have
twenty minutes,' he told her coldly, closing the door
behind him.

A glance in the long mirror before Lisa ventured
downstairs told her three things—that the dress was of
an excellent style and fit, that it looked good and, most
of all, that it was quite unsuitable for a routine evening
meal in a private house.

Its neckline was too low, the sleevelessness too
revealing of long, bare arms. She shrugged away the
doubts. It was the only ankle-length dress she had
brought with her.

The eyes of the young woman seated at the extreme
end of a four-seater settee had no doubts about the
unsuitability of the dress, either. Lisa entered the room,
noting that the door was open.

'Come in,' the young woman invited. 'I take it you're
Alexander's new secretary? And there's no need to look
so puzzled. You've seen me many times—on magazine
covers, inside glossies, at fashion shows if you've ever
attended them.'

'I do remember, Miss Allen. I've always admired
your beauty.' Lisa had spoken with such sincerity, the
compliment was not turned away with a sarcastic
comment from the recipient. It was the imperious head
that turned its profile towards Lisa, as if the woman
simply didn't want to know.

Maybe, Lisa thought, she would rather forget her
modelling days now she's Zander's fiancée. And why
had she called him Alexander, for heaven's sake?

'That dress you're wearing is completely unsuitable
for dining with us. Did you think you were going to a
charity dinner, in the presence of the town's top
people?' The question was insulting, but Lisa found it
difficult to prevent a smile from curving her lips.

'I'm sorry about this,' Lisa looked down at herself,

'but when I packed to come here, I wasn't aware of the rule.'

'What rule?' Zander's fiancée asked sharply. Lisa indicated the hem of her dress. 'Who told you it was a rule?'

'Z—— Mr Cameron,' she corrected hastily.

'Did you want me?' The question came impersonally from the doorway. Lisa swung round, her colour rising.

'No, I——'

Corinna Allen cut across Lisa's halting explanation. 'Darling,' her hand was extended invitingly, 'Miss Maynard was answering my question. She was saying you'd told her the rules.'

Lisa and Zander exchanged glances. She knew he was remembering how they had broken the rules only about thirty minutes ago.

He crossed the room, indicating to Lisa that she should sit down. He took the proffered hand, manicured to perfection, and bent, at his fiancée's prompting, to kiss her cheek. She patted the empty cushion beside her. 'Sit next to me, darling. I've been feeling neglected all day.'

'Sorry about that,' Zander commented, standing behind her and letting his hands slide down to the shoulders which sloped so attractively beneath the silky but high-necked dinner gown.

Corinna threw back her head so that she could look up into his face. 'Mm, that's nice. Massage me, darling, I feel the need to relax.'

It was the attention she wanted, Lisa decided sourly, the display of affection. She already looked as relaxed as a curled-up cat. Her long, fair hair had been brushed so that it shone to match the light in her eyes.

Lisa wanted to run from the room instead of being forced to watch Zander smiling into his fiancée's eyes. The dress she wore, Lisa estimated, must have cost a small fortune—Zander's, probably. Desperately, Lisa wished she could dissociate herself from the muted love scene going on in front of her agonised eyes.

Trying to discover Zander's feelings from his expression was like attempting to read a letter while it was still inside the envelope. And did that dress have to reveal his woman's every soft and lissom curve, every enticing aspect of that body which, in itself, must have been worth a king's ransom to its possessor during her years of modelling?

'Darling,' there was a plaintive note in Corinna's voice, 'you're hurting me!' She caught at one of Zander's hands as he started to remove them. 'Were you thinking about your horrid business worries and having them out on me?'

Lisa looked up quickly to find, with a shock, that his gaze was fixed on her.

'I was thinking of my business worries,' he answered shortly. 'Lisa, would you like a drink?'

'Darling,' the husky voice complained, 'isn't it usual to ask your fiancée first?'

His smile was gentle as he took the outstretched hand in his. 'My apologies, Corinna. But I know your tastes so well, it was hardly necessary for me to ask, was it?'

Lisa wondered where he had hidden such smooth talk while he had gone around with her, when he had been bearded and tanned, tough in mind as well as muscle. Nor had there been the merest touch of silkiness in either his tone or action in their dealings since. But she had never been a blonde-haired, green-eyed beauty, nor had her picture been featured in magazines and television advertisements.

'Lisa?' There it was again, the briskness, and it hit her all the harder for having followed on the assumed suavity with which he had addressed his fiancée. 'You didn't answer me. Do you want your usu——' In time, he checked himself and Lisa breathed again.

'Yes, please——' She caught her breath before his shortened name had come breaking through, crossing her fingers that Corinna had noticed nothing. It seemed she had not.

'Why do you say her name,' her eyes slid to Lisa, 'as if she were——' a small frown marred the flawless face, 'were someone special to you?'

Trying to convey a warning, Lisa sought Zander's eyes. He had gone to the drinks table, leaving the question on her doorstep! 'I suppose,' she offered tentatively, 'that someone's secretary is always—well, just a little—special, don't you think, Miss Allen?'

Corinna still seemed puzzled. 'He called Shirley by her name, but the way he said it was just—ordinary, somehow.'

A drink was handed to her and she thanked her fiancé with a seductive flash of her eyes. Lisa could not see Zander's response, since his back was to her. For heaven's sake, she thought, trying desperately not to frown and clenching her teeth instead, how long can I keep this up, this pretence of an employee's indifference to her boss's electrifying presence?

This man isn't only my boss—she was talking silently to herself—he's almost my lover, isn't he? So how does he expect me to feel nothing, care nothing for him? To pretend, in front of his wife-to-be, that we hadn't met before I became his secretary?

He was standing in front of her, waiting patiently for her to emerge from her tortured reveries. Startled, her head jerked up. Their eyes met and she knew that hers were pleading with him to release her from her emotional bondage and find another girl to take her place.

His were a glinting brown, hinting at intimacy and disavowing it at the same time. There came from him an invisible yet near-palpable force as if he were making savage love to her, compelling her to surrender, then walking away as if he had not touched her.

When her hand finally reached the glass, it was shaking. For a second he held it with her, steadying it. 'Thank you,' she said, keeping her eyes firmly on the liquid until it was lowered and held by both her hands.

'I think,' Zander commented casually, 'my secretary's thoughts must have been far away.' He moved back to sit beside his fiancée. 'Recalling your holiday, maybe? Where was it that you went—Lanzarote, did you say?'

It was impossible to look at the man who was baiting her so mercilessly. Had she done so, she would have given away to the watching, waiting girl beside him all her most precious secrets and longings. And anger at

the man who had so misled her while on that holiday
would not have been far behind.

'Isn't that an island in the Canaries?' Corinna asked.

Lisa was relieved to hear the question, since it
revealed that any suspicions which Corinna might have
entertained about the short but strange silence must
have been dispersed by Zander's comments.

'You've been there recently, darling,' Corinna
observed, 'haven't you? Curious that you didn't meet. It
can't be a very large place.'

'We wouldn't have known each other, Miss Allen,
even if we had,' Lisa put in quickly.

'But you work for the same company,' her hand
motioned from one to the other, 'obviously.'

'A large company, remember,' Zander returned
easily, resting his head against the back of the couch.
'Lisa was in a very different section of it. She dealt with
the human side—recruitment, welfare, staff problems.'

Lisa nodded vigorously—a little too vigorously? she
wondered. 'Personnel. We found people temporary
accommodation, even helping to straighten out their
private problems, sometimes. I enjoyed it.'

'Then why did you leave the department?'

Corinna's coolly asked question almost floored her.
She looked at Zander, but his head was back, eyes
closed, mouth curved in a let-her-deal-with-that smile.

'Orders of the boss,' she answered, her eyes flashing
victory as his eyes came open.

He was not thrown by the ball hitting him instead of
the ground as it flew over the net. 'I needed a new
secretary,' he took her up. 'I made discreet enquiries as
to the qualities of the existing secretaries. I received a
glowing reference about Lisa from Miss Harris, and
here she is——' A sly glance at the girl in question was
followed by the ambiguous statement, 'glowing for me.'

Corinna did not appear to notice the strained silence
that followed. Her hand rested on Zander's knee.
'Darling,' she asked, swinging her long, fair hair and
flashing her eyes, 'would you be a lamb and get me my
folder of photographs?'

Lisa found the length of her own nails of immense

interest. Somehow she had to keep the smile from her face. In no circumstances could she imagine Zander acting the 'lamb' to anyone. She waited to hear the words, 'You could get them yourself, Corinna,' or something equally reducing.

To her astonishment, Zander did indeed play 'the lamb' and produce the required folder from a magazine rack.

'Miss Maynard,' the voice was imperious this time, 'my specs are over there. I should like to have them, please.'

Lisa was too surprised to do anything else but obey the order. It hadn't even been a request, she fumed, as she delivered them to their owner.

'Now sit here, on the arm of the couch next to me, and look at these.'

Was this unbelievable sense of her own importance the result of being engaged to Alexander Cameron, top executive of Thistle International? Was this overbearing despotism a characteristic which Zander really wanted in the woman who was to be his wife?

If so, she thought, forcing herself to feel thankful, it's just as well events took the course they did. I've had a lucky escape. But she hadn't escaped, and she knew it. He had taken her heart when he had gone from her and he hadn't even known.

Perched on the arm of the couch, she looked with frank admiration at the photographs which revealed the beauty of the features and form of the model, Corinna Allen. 'I had these copies made. They were made for a reason.' Closing her long-lashed eyes, she held the folder to her as if it were something precious.

Lisa returned to her seat. 'I just can't understand,' she remarked, 'how you could ever bring yourself to give it all up.'

Zander stiffened. She actually saw his muscles tense. Corinna's head swung towards her. 'Don't you know?' she asked. 'Do you really not know?'

Lisa shook her head. 'I have no idea, Miss Allen.' Why had her heart started beating so much faster?

There was a tap at the door, and Edgar's head came

round it. 'Milly says dinner is served, Mr Cameron, Miss Allen.' Then he withdrew.

Eyes on Lisa, Zander rose. Lisa stood, too, trying to puzzle out the curious message in his look. He went, not to lead his fiancée to the door, but to go past her and bend behind the couch. He straightened, holding two crutches.

Lisa's hand went to her throat. She felt stifled, her breathing restricted, as she watched his actions. He caught his fiancée under the armpits. Gently, slowly, he eased her up, holding her by the waist while he pushed a crutch under one arm, then the other.

Corinna gazed at Lisa with a kind of twisted defiance. 'Now is your question answered?' she queried bitterly. With an upward look at Zander, she made her slow and painful way to the door.

CHAPTER EIGHT

IF it had not been for Corinna's flow of talk, interrupted only by her pause for Zander's replies, or to eat her food, it would have been a silent meal.

Lisa scarcely spoke. Shock had affected her so deeply she spent most of the meal lost in a gaudy, raucous mental underworld, her plunge into which had knocked her reason sideways.

Zander was engaged to a woman who had been disabled in some terrible accident. Thus, he was tied to her more securely than if she had been in full health. When they married—Lisa's eyes closed momentarily and in despair—any intimate life they shared would be greatly altered by Corinna's disability.

That was, she reflected, unable to deflect the bombardment of her brain by the tormenting thoughts, if Corinna allowed the normal intimacies of marriage. She herself knew how deep were Zander's desires. She knew, also, of his passionate nature. After his marriage, what would he do? Her eyes lifted involuntarily to find that his gaze was on her.

Had he made contact with her thought waves and thus knew exactly what she was thinking? Or did her face, even her sombre silence, give them away?

'Lost your appetite, Lisa?' he asked. There was a taunting in his tone that made her bridle.

Having discovered yet again how unscrupulously he had deceived her after they had first met, her bitterness against him was steadily mounting.

'I wasn't aware that I had, Mr Cameron,' she retorted, continuing doggedly to finish the course even though the others were waiting. 'You worked me so hard when I arrived, you sapped me of energy.' Her smile was meant to pierce his armour, but it seemed not even to have touched it. 'I'm just taking my time,' she added, 'in replenishing my energy quotient.'

The answering smile that tugged at his mouth brought small flares into her cheeks. The moment she had finished, Corinna spoke.

'I notice that Miss Maynard hasn't yet asked me how my accident happened and why it turned me into a cripple.'

Lisa flinched at the word, as it seemed Corinna had intended. 'You're not a cripple, Miss Allen. You're beautiful and you're young. You might even be cured——'

'I'll never be cured.' Her voice rang with some emotion Lisa could not identify. 'There'll be no marital relationship between Zander and myself after we're married. Do you know, I could see from your expression that that was the first thing you thought of.'

In vain, Lisa shook her head, looking appealingly at Zander. His watchful brown eyes did not flicker from hers, but they held no readable message.

'And what will he do?' Corinna persisted, after Milly had hurried in to remove the first course plates and serve the sweet. 'Turn to other women as most normal men would?'

Lisa searched again for the brown eyes, having first, she hoped, removed all expression from hers. They had not moved from her face, but still she found no answer in them.

'I can tell you now,' the hard, unbeautiful voice went on, 'that he won't. He's an honourable man, Miss Maynard. Given any opportunity to sleep with a woman, he'll turn away, remembering he's a married man.'

In despair now, Lisa begged Zander silently to interrupt the flow of corrosive acid from his fiancée's lips. Wasn't it burning him as it was herself? He did nothing but look at her, although she noticed his eyes had hardened.

'Once his wedding ring is on my finger,' Corinna went on, pushing away her untouched sweet, 'he has such high principles, he would rather suffer the agonies of celibacy than indulge his frustrated desires.'

There was a heavy silence. Lisa attempted to eat her

sweet, but she could force no more than half of it down
her throat, tempting though it was. She pushed it from
her, pulled it back, crumpled her table napkin, unfolded it.

All her actions were watched closely by the beautiful
creature seated opposite. 'Have I trodden on your
sensibilities, Miss Maynard? If so, I must apologise, but
I've only been telling you the truth.'

'Are you trying to punish your fiancé, Miss Allen?'
The words of the question hit the walls and shot back,
like ricocheting bullets. 'Has he committed some
terrible crime for which he must be made to pay for the
rest of his life?'

Corinna's pale skin became inflamed with a terrible
fury. 'Tell that girl to go, Alexander. I will not take one
more word of her insolence!'

Turning to him, Corinna groped for him blindly. He
moved his chair and held her while she sobbed against
his shoulder. His hand stroked her hair, his hard lips
softened to murmur private endearments.

Lisa thrust back her chair. 'I'm sorry, Miss Allen, I'm
so terribly sorry.' She swung round and raced to the
door. Halting, she said, 'I'll pack my things and leave,
Mr Cameron. What I said was unforgivable.'

'It was unforgivable, Miss Maynard,' his words sliced
into her, 'but you will stay. You're here as my secretary,
not as a guest.'

Outside the room, Lisa found she was shaking. There
was no visible sign of it—she studied her hand—so the
trembling was all inside her. Or was it her world
tumbling about her ears? The last of her dreams—
dreams she did not even realise she still cherished—had
smashed to pieces around her.

All the time they must have persisted, even from the
moment of Zander's leaving her with Myra and Phil on
that holiday island in the sun. Dreams that one day
there would be no barriers between them and that, in
the final analysis, they would be free to come together.

It was growing dark and she was sitting in the sun
chalet. Milly had told her Mr Cameron wouldn't mind
at all. Miss Shirley, when she used to come, had often

used the chalet, but in the daytime when the sun was shining, not when it was dark, Milly had added, smiling.

'It's a lovely place to go if you want a bit of peace and quiet. Mr Cameron takes himself there at all times of the day, not to mention the middle of the night,' Milly had told her.

A fact, Lisa considered, resting her head back on the cushioned wooden bench seat, which told a tale all of its own. The chalet had been fixed into position to catch the rays of the afternoon sun.

Now, she basked in moonlight. It shed shades and shadows which were kinder to the troubled heart than the sun's harsher glow. She had come for the tranquillity which, from the moment she had seen it, this place had seemed to offer.

Closing her eyes, she breathed deeply of the night-scents, heard the occasional flip of pool water against the sides, the hum of busy night insects. Even with such serenity all around, she could not find a way of using it as a soothing balm.

Nothing could take away the scorching knowledge that Corinna's disability bound Zander to her more surely than any other kind of tie. Yet he had not told her, had kept her in ignorance of everything. For this she could not forgive him, since he knew—how could he not?—how deeply she had fallen in love with him in their earlier acquaintance.

With the darkness acting like a projector screen, she was back in that dark cave walking beside the subterranean pool which caught the light coming in from the fissures in the rock above. Zander had told her how the clear waters were illuminated by them according to the angle of the sun's rays.

Now she sat in a sun chalet, feeling cold in the moonlight. A shiver took hold, shaking her from head to foot. Opening her eyes, she saw a man's figure outlined in the darkness at the entrance. She swallowed the scream and her breathing levelled out as she recognised the head-shape and body pattern of the newcomer.

Only Zander had that proud stance, strength of
shoulder and leanness of flesh possessed by no other
man of her acquaintance. He had frightened her and
her belligerence lingered, making her snap,

'What do you want?'

He said nothing, so she probed,

'To find me? To fire me? To tear me to bits for my
attitude to your fiancée?'

His stride brought him in one up the steps, in two to
seat himself beside her on the bench.

'Wrong three times. I came for the thing I usually
find here. Peace and silence, an escape from the
demands life constantly makes on me.'

Lisa stood up. 'I'm sorry, I didn't realise. I'll leave
you to your peace and quiet——'

His hand shot out, gripping her arm. 'You'll stay
right here. Sit down!'

'I refuse to let you bark orders at me as if I were a
rebellious child!' She could not free herself no matter
how she shook her arm. 'Nor will I sit anywhere near
you.'

Zander pulled so hard on her arm she fell back on to
the bench, hurting her back. The impact winded her
and she caught her breath in pain. Bending forward and
holding her head, she felt a massaging hand moving
across her back.

'Don't,' she moaned, 'don't touch me!'

He ignored her statement and, against her will, she
found herself relaxing. His massaging action was
soothing, yet stirring her, rekindling the strength of
feeling which had been fired to life in that mysterious,
alien-landscaped island where they had met.

'Please stop,' the request was a whisper now and she
was looking into his face, seeking for his features but
seeing only shadows cast by the moon's light. 'I want
nothing to do with you, do you understand?'

Her rejection of him this time had the desired effect.
He rested back, hands slipped into his waistband, legs
outstretched. 'Tell me more,' he invited cuttingly.

'So many lies you told me,' she protested, 'yet you
pretend you did nothing wrong?'

'I told you no lies, Lisa.'

'You acted them. You can't deny that, no matter how often I challenge you about it. And you lied, too, by omitting to tell me the truth.'

After a long silence, he responded, 'Our relationship was at no time more than a temporary thing. At the time—and *you* can't deny this—you accepted the fact unconditionally. So what concern was it of yours how truthful or otherwise I was about my personal life?'

'No concern of mine—yet it *was*. How could it not have been when we—you know what happened between us.' He did not move a muscle in response. She turned on him, hitting his thigh with her fist. 'We made love, didn't we, we made love?'

He caught her wrist and threw it from him.

'We went places together,' she persisted, her voice wavering, 'we danced, we kissed. We lay on the sands on the edge of the sea. We made love.' She was whispering now, as the memories returned like an incoming tide. 'I slept in your arms in my bed. I——' her fingers gripped his thigh, shaking it, 'I let you get nearer to me in every way than any other man I've known.'

His fingers were stilling her action. 'That was your decision.'

'How can you stay so cool? It meant nothing to you, did it? Did it?'

He grasped her other hand and dragged her closer, turning her so that she lay across him. Putting both of her wrists in one of his hands, he put his other over her mouth.

'I've had it up to my neck. I've taken tears and a verbal onslaught from Corinna, I've had my impotent future displayed and held up for public inspection. I've taken accusations and attacks on my integrity from you.' He grasped a bunch of her hair. 'Now I'm going to prove to me, as well as to you, that I still possess my masculinity.'

Lisa shook her head, only to bite her lip at the pain. 'I will not be your mistress. I refuse to be used by you. You can't make me, Zander, you can't!'

He ignored her outburst, and caught her hands again, using his free hand to jerk down the narrowed bands of fabric which formed the shoulder straps of her dress. Her breasts were revealed and the softness of the audacious lips laid a burning trail downwards. As her physical excitement increased, her head fell back to hang, hair brushing the wooden arm of the bench.

'No, no,' she breathed, 'Zander, I can't stand it!'

There was a low, malicious laugh and cold fingers of fear played a tune along her spine. His mouth reached the rose-tipped sensitivity, teasing, kissing until the hardening flesh became his to do with it whatever he desired.

He released her hands, knowing her resistance had gone. Blindly, Lisa reached upward for his face, rubbing her palm over the evening roughness of a cheek, then finding his hair and gripping.

Her thighs began to come alive under his slow caresses and she moaned, 'No, Zander, please, *please*! Stop, oh, stop . . .' Her mouth was dry and she tried moistening it with her tongue. 'We mustn't go on. I'd have to leave, I could never work for you again.'

It seemed that at last she had found the key to his reason. His head lifted and a shaft of moonlight showed her the wild hunger of his expression. His gaze moved down her pliant body, then, as if he were almost maddened by his unfulfilled need, he brought down his lips on her mouth.

He lifted her with the strong band of his arm until she was sitting across him. Her arms met behind his neck and accepted his savage plundering of her mouth, taking the deep, deep kisses until her body lay like a rag doll in his merciless hold.

Finally he stopped and her cheek sought his chest. His forehead lowered to rest on her hair. So they remained for a long time, stirring only when a draught of cool air caused Lisa to shiver. Zander lifted his head, saw the disarrangement of her clothes and replaced each shoulder strap. Then he put her beside him, running a hand over his hair.

'Will you go in first, please?' he said at last. His voice

was so controlled and so neutral her heart sank to hear it.

'Won't Milly see me, or Edgar?'

'They'll be in their room. I'll follow almost behind you. They'll hear me and Edgar will come down to lock up.'

Lisa stood up, her legs weak, her head throbbing. 'Do you still want me to stay?'

'I want you to stay,' he answered, his voice empty of emotion.

'Then I'll stay. Goodnight, Zander.'

He did not answer, but a few moments later she heard his footsteps following.

Zander had finished and gone at breakfast time when Lisa came down. Corinna was on to toast and marmalade with the morning's paper folded beside her. Her upward glance took in not only Lisa's lingering fatigue after an unsatisfactory night's sleep, but also her simply-styled dark-blue dress. It was the examination of an expert in fashion and modelling rather than one which sprang from a wish to make the subject of it feel small.

Lisa took comfort from the fact that there was no sulkiness or pique in the young woman's expression. In fact, Lisa reasoned, she seemed surprisingly resilient character-wise.

Milly carried in a steaming plate of eggs and bacon, placing it in front of Lisa. 'All right for you, Miss Lisa?' she asked. 'You don't mind me calling you that, do you, dear? I called the other young lady Miss Shirley.'

'I don't mind at all, Milly.' The housekeeper hurried out. While Corinna continued reading the newspaper, Lisa tucked into her breakfast. She was, she discovered, surprisingly hungry.

Corinna drank some coffee, watching Lisa as she ate. 'You seem to be enjoying that.' Lisa nodded, managing a smile. The events of the evening before were still too clear in her mind to allow the smile to be warm.

Corinna folded the paper and put it aside. Her hair hung loose, giving her an intriguing touch of freshness and youth, both of which, Lisa considered, she must long ago have left behind. As a result of her injury, she had plainly lost a great deal—a career, mobility, independence, yet the hint of young beauty which rose from the face of the girl in those photographs she seemed to cherish, still miraculously remained.

Lisa found that it was difficult, in the circumstances, to be honest with herself where this fiancée of Zander's was concerned, but she had to admit that she understood the woman's attraction for him.

'I never did tell you,' Corinna was saying, 'how my accident happened, did I?' Lisa shook her head, extracting toast from the rack and spreading it with the yeast extract which reposed in a jar on the table.

'I was mad about horse-riding.' Corinna clasped her hands and rested her chin on them in a pose she must have adopted many times in her professional past. 'I thought I knew it all. One morning—it was a beautiful day—I went out in a kind of mad mood. You know how these moods happen?'

Lisa nodded, pouring herself coffee and offering some to her companion, who shook her head.

'I started off sedately enough, then something got into me and I pushed the horse into a gallop. Noble must have caught my mood. He obeyed my instructions, more than obeyed them, leaping hedges on the Cameron estate—it's a large one—going high over gates. It was at one of those where it happened. Noble hadn't taken into account—I mean, he couldn't, could he?—that the ground on the other side dipped down and was deeply rutted.'

Lisa stopped eating and stared at the lovely, unlined face. 'The horse fell?'

Corinna nodded. 'I was thrown. My spine has never been the same since. It took months before the other parts of me had healed enough for me to use them normally. My legs, I was told, would take much, much longer. There is an operation, they said, that they could try, but they couldn't guarantee success.'

'You didn't have it?'

'I'd had enough of operations to last me a lifetime. If

they could have told me it would definitely succeed, I would have had it.' She lifted her sloping shoulders and lowered them unhappily.

'Were you alone when it happened?' asked Lisa.

There was a pause before the answer came. 'No, I wasn't alone. Someone else—was there.'

It was plain the tale had come to an end. The identity of that 'someone else' was to remain a secret. Lisa took a very inspired guess as to who that person was. Zander and Corinna must already have been engaged, and the accident must have cemented that relationship in so many complex ways.

Lisa stood up with the intention of going to her office. Corinna halted her, asking, 'Would you please give me that handbell on the table over there? Zander is usually here to make sure I have it, but he seemed to have lost his appetite this morning and only drank a cup of coffee.'

And I know why, Lisa thought, trying to quell the sense of hopelessness which threatened to bring down her spirits. She handed the bell to Corinna, experiencing a sense of compassion now that she knew the cause of the woman's imperiousness, as she had regarded such orders yesterday.

'Do you ring that for help?' Lisa asked.

'When I want assistance with getting up or moving.' Her smile seemed to be an effort. 'A bit primitive in the electronic age, but when I use it, Edgar comes running.'

'I'll call him, if you like,' Lisa offered, but Corinna shook her head, returning to reading the newspaper.

Zander was at his desk when Lisa arrived. He looked up briefly and her heart went out to him as she saw the deep shadows around his eyes. The look of steel they wore soon took away her sorrow, replacing it with a rigid anger. As if she had been to blame for the events in the sun chalet . . .

'I'm sorry I'm late, Mr Cameron,' she remarked, approaching his desk.

'I'm early,' he replied curtly. 'I've no work for you at present, so there's no need for you to hang around in here.'

He had intended to offend. A retort sprang to her lips, but she pressed them together. He saw the suppressed anger, but his blank expression did not alter.

As she reached the door, he told her, 'You'll find the morning's post on your desk. Open it, answer what you can and bring the rest to me.'

'Yes, Mr Cameron.' Was he inciting her to rebel, so that he could put her in her place?

She went through the door dividing his room from hers and rested her head back against it. Already there was a deep-down throb of pain. How much longer could she stand it? Last night she had told him she would stay. In the cold light of morning, the promise seemed almost impossible to keep.

While she worked, she heard the murmur of voices from Zander's room. The place had been strangely quiet when she had worked there after her arrival yesterday. Now it seemed that people were calling in.

Having finished all the letters she could answer without advice, Lisa lifted one of the telephones on her desk and asked, 'Mr Cameron?'

Somebody laughed at the other end, saying, 'You've got through to me, dear—Milly. Sometimes Miss Shirley did that by mistake. You're on the white phone, aren't you? Well, the yellow one's for one of the other offices, that is, the one Mr Cameron's father uses when he visits here, and the red one will connect you with Mr Cameron himself.'

Lisa smiled. 'Thanks for telling me, Milly. I'll make a note of that.'

Lifting the red telephone, she heard the clatter at the other end and waited for someone to speak. Afraid that she might again have been connected to the wrong person, she continued to wait.

'What the hell are you playing at?' she was asked. 'You know who I am. What do you want?'

Lisa contained her fury at his quite unreasonable attitude and answered, 'I'm sorry to be so dull-witted, Mr Cameron, but if Milly hadn't told me, I wouldn't have known I was speaking to you.'

'Please overlook my unforgivable omission to give

you a lecture on the telephone links on your desk,' was his cutting reply. 'If you don't tell me what you want quickly, I will personally come in and wring your neck!'

The prospect of having his hands anywhere on her body forced up the pace of her heartbeat, but she steadied it, answering, 'I've finished all I can do without your further instructions.'

'So what are you waiting for? Come right in.' There was the touch of silkiness again which she had heard directed last night at his fiancée. This time, for her, it was laced with sarcasm.

Closing his door behind her, she stayed there for a few moments. He looked her over in the kind of way that had her heart leaping, yet at the same time made her feel classified, in his mind, as 'easy-to-get'. Grinding her teeth, yet hiding them behind her closed lips, she walked slowly across to him.

'Will you please sign these, Mr Cameron?' she said, putting the folder of typed letters in front of him.

As he scrawled his signature across each one, she folded them into their envelopes. He came to those which needed his personal attention. One was so long and detailed, she knew it would take him some time to take in each point and come to a conclusion about them.

Her eyes lifted to the windows. 'What a beautiful view you have!' The words came from her spontaneously and she went across to stare out across the rise and fall of flourishing green fields, the gentle hills topped here and there by clumps of trees. For some time Lisa gazed, lost in the quiet, soothing beauty of the surrounding landscape. She wished she could steal some of that tranquillity and infuse it into herself. A sigh escaped her.

Hands descended to her shoulders, startling her and creating a sense of guilt that, in her mind, she had gone too far away from work and all its attendant problems.

Zander turned her and his touch was like a lightning-strike. The rigid lines of his jaw had softened. His eyes had lost their hardness, lighting his face.

'What has happened to your smile?'

Lisa shook her head, unable to bring herself to meet the tenderness of his expression.

Roughened fingers lifted her chin. 'Your laughter's gone, too, my winsome wee thing.' His fingers trailed her cheek, making her shiver.

He had quoted Robert Burns, and in these circumstances, too! Deliberately, he had brought back memories of their holiday loving ... She couldn't stand it, that he should be so unfeeling, even, it seemed, regarding their passionate island encounter as something amusing, to smile at now that it was safely behind them.

As she twisted away, her eyes darkened with the depth of her anger. '*You* took my smiles away, *you* stole my laughter! I might just have been able to look back on that episode as—as a passing infatuation and forgotten it, if you hadn't deceived me in so many ways.' He would never know how far from the truth that statement was. Infatuation, when she had fallen deeply in love with him?

'So you're back to calling me a liar.' His voice was almost weary, yet the rigidity of his jaw was back, and the hardness had returned to his eyes.

'Those compliments you paid me, and that nonsense about loving my smile. You only said those things to get what you wanted. Yet your fiancée called you an honourable man!' The sneer in her voice and eyes were meant to be there. 'She should have been in the sun chalet last night. She should have seen you with me on the island, *and in my bed!*'

Zander was standing beside his desk, hand slipped into jacket pocket. 'And did I not act honourably then?' He approached her and his fingers closed cruelly over her upper arm. 'Who virtually begged me to take her? Who said to me, "Yes, oh yes"?' Her eyes clouded at the memory, and pain shot through her, not only at his bruising fingers but at the condemnation in his eyes.

'Please,' she tried to move his fingers, 'you're hurting! Let me go!'

'You didn't say that then, did you?' he queried savagely. 'It was I who exercised incredible self-control, all things considered. I was the one who said you'd

remember me as the man who had held back of his own
accord. Just imagine, if I'd gone on as my body urged
me to do—plus the woman beside me—you might, just,
have been expecting my child. What would my fiancée
have had to say about things then?'

'You didn't tell me about her, did you?' she accused
fiercely, jerking to free herself and wincing at the pain
when he let her go. 'If I'd known of her existence, I
wouldn't have spoken a single word to you from the
start, let alone allow to happen—what did happen.'

He went to stand at the other window. When he
turned back at last, Lisa was by the desk, flipping
through the sealed envelopes. His mood was dark.

Reaching out for the pile of letters he had been
reading, he told her, 'I'll dictate replies to these into the
machine. Go back to your room and I'll ring when I
want you.'

'But I can take dictation, Mr Cameron.'

'Do you think I don't know that?' His eyes were
searing as they caught up with hers. 'I just want you out
of here.'

Lisa's breathing quickened to hold back the surge of
emotion at his curt dismissal, but she turned at the
door. 'The long dress I wore last night——'

'I suppose you're going to tell me I tore it. I'll pay for
a replacement.'

'No, thank you. I wouldn't accept anything from
you, except my salary.' There was a sound like steel
clashing as their eyes met, but Lisa knew it had only
been in her head. 'I was going to ask permission to go
shopping for something more suitable to wear at
dinner.'

He waved a hand as if it was of no consequence to
him what she did with her time. 'Take this afternoon
off. Can you drive? You can? Take the small car in the
second garage. It's really Corinna's, but it's been kept
in good condition by a devoted Edgar.'

It was Edgar, too, who gave her a set of car keys,
escorted her to the small red car and explained the
controls. It took her only a few minutes to grasp them.
She praised the shining exterior of the car and was told

by a proud Edgar that the car's engine and its other
workings were in just as good a state.

'It's only a five-minute drive to Churwood,' Edgar
informed her. 'You could have walked if you'd only
been going there.'

'I may not find what I want,' she answered. 'If not,
what do you suggest I do?'

'Carry on to Witney,' Edgar advised. 'There are some
nice little shops there, Milly says. But there's a lady's
shop in Churwood that Miss Corinna thinks the world
of.'

Lisa waved her thanks and drove down the long
driveway to the road. If Corinna patronises the shop,
she was thinking, as she turned into the quiet roadway,
it's sure to be way above my means, especially as
Zander probably pays for everything she buys.

Lisa walked around the small, busy town, hearing the
church clock strike three. For a while she just
wandered, crossing roads which were just wide enough
for two cars to pass, looking in antique shops, walking
up and down the town's hills.

Finding the shop to which Edgar had referred, she
gazed in the windows and sighed to see that all the price
tags had been turned from view. Entering, she found a
welcome in the smile of the woman who came to greet
her and who, she guessed, was the owner.

Her fears about the prices had not been entirely
fulfilled, since there were in stock a selection of less
expensive garments, the kind Corinna would not waste
her time looking at, Lisa decided.

'There are those,' the owner remarked, sorting
through the dresses on a rail, 'who won't buy anything
that doesn't bear a famous name tag. Of course, I don't
stop them. I don't tell them you could get just as good a
quality and style by paying less, minus the famous
name, but,' she selected a dress, 'I am telling you.'

Lisa found her smile so disarming, she forgave the
sales talk and tried on the dress. It was a dark blue,
fitted her perfectly and possessed a rounded neckline
and half-length sleeves.

'You could,' the woman advised, 'wear any kind of

necklace to dress up the neck, or a bangle or two to
decorate the space between your wrists and the sleeves.
Or,' with another smile, 'with your lovely skin and fresh
looks, just wear yourself, as it were, simply and
unaffectedly.'

'Thank you, I'll have this,' Lisa told her, 'and I
compliment you on being an excellent saleswoman.'

The owner laughed, accepting the credit card. 'I'm
here to sell my stock, I admit, but I also want to please
my customers so that they come back asking for more.'

'Now,' said Lisa, looking round, 'I think I might look
at a long skirt and one or two tops.' Then she joined in
the woman's laughter.

Laden with bags, Lisa walked towards the car park.
Her mouth was dry and she felt in need of refreshment.
The parcels she carried made that impossible, she
decided. Turning a corner from the main street, she
almost bumped into someone coming from the other
direction. The corner of the building had hidden each
from the other.

He was tall and her heart danced in anticipation but
its jig came to an abrupt end. This man was not dark,
with brown eyes so penetrating they could almost read
her thoughts. His hair was fair, his skin suntanned, and
it took her a few seconds to place him.

'Well,' he said, eyeing her face and whatever he could
see of her figure, with the look of an expert, 'if it isn't
one of Alexander Cameron's little peccadilloes!'

'Reg Beckley?' Lisa asked, her heart responding as if
she had seen a tornado approaching. 'You're a long
way from your Canary Islands development project.'

He shook his head slowly, making a 'no-but-guess-
again' sound. 'Look,' as someone tried to pass, 'we're in
the way here. Let's go somewhere for a thirst-quencher,
okay? I'll take a couple of your bags, shall I?' He did
not wait for her answer. 'I know a nice little place just
down there.' He pointed to an inn sign. 'They serve tea
on request. It's called The Bell, and in licensing hours,
it's a pub.'

'Which is why you know it?' asked Lisa, with a
sideways smile.

'Maybe,' he grinned. 'I don't live round here. I just visit when the occasion demands.'

They sat on a low couch under wooden beams in a room which led to the bar, closed until the evening. The walls displayed old prints of the area in decades and centuries past. A couple of friendly dogs nosed their way around the strange feet and on hearing Lisa's soft encouragement and feeling her stroking hand, went away satisfied.

The order was taken and quickly served in a friendly, easy way. The pieces of shortbread looked homemade. Shortbread—it reminded her of Zander and his Scottish inheritance. It also gave her conscience a jolt. She shouldn't be there, really, sitting and drinking with a man who was to her, after all, only a stranger.

More important, she should have returned to work. Except that her boss had practically thrown her out of the place, implying she could go where she liked except stay in his presence.

'Something troubling you?' asked Reg Beckley, taking the tea she had poured him.

'Maybe,' was her far from encouraging reply. Turning the subject from herself, she asked, 'So you're back from your sojourn in the moonscape island of Lanzarote?'

'For a while.' With a sly grin, he added, 'You haven't asked me yet, what am I doing in these parts? I could ask the same of you.'

'It's a long story,' she answered, taking a crumbling bite of shortbread.

'Agreed. London's some distance from here, isn't it, including the big, big offices of Thistle International.'

Lisa chewed thoughtfully. 'How do you know where Thistle's U.K. offices are? You work for a rival consortium.'

He downed his tea and held the cup out for more. 'Do I? That's news to me.'

'You don't mean that you——' she stabbed an unbelieving finger towards him, 'work for them? And that all the time I was getting—getting friendly with Z—— Mr Cameron on my holiday, you knew I worked for Thistle, yet didn't tell me that you did, too? Nor did you tell me that Mr Cameron was my employer?' He smiled, picking up shortbread crumbs from his plate with a dampened finger. 'No wonder you called him "boss"! I asked Z—— Mr Cameron why, and he wouldn't tell me.'

'Of course he wouldn't. That would have spoiled his sport, wouldn't it? Stopped the cat playing with his tame little mouse. And look, sg ahead, call him Zander. I know all about your affair.'

'It wasn't an affair,' Lisa denied defensively. She drained her second cup of tea and darted a glance at the man, hoping he had not heard the small note of fear.

'It wasn't?' He pretended astonishment. 'What was it then, a hand-holding, kiss-me-only-on-the-cheek thing?' Another angled look came her way. 'And him sleeping with you, too.'

Her head shot round. 'How did you——' She checked, horrified at what she had given away. 'We didn't—I mean, it was only . . . Why should I explain to you?'

'You don't have to. I'm too well informed about our employer's—shall we say—activities where women are concerned to need to be told anything about that side of him.'

Lisa would have held her head if the action would not have betrayed to him her intense concern. 'Did he—Zander—tell you about us?' If he had let her down so badly as to discuss her with his employees . . .

'He didn't have to. That bit about sleeping with you was a guess on my part. Just seeing you two together told me—anyone, in fact—all they wanted to know.'

'Have you told anybody else?' asked Lisa.

'You mean grafted the information on to the company grapevine, so to speak? Not yet.' He stood up, rang the small hand bell and paid. Lisa fought down her rising panic at his words and smiled her thanks at the woman who had served them. Reg Beckley picked up the parcels and Lisa held her share.

'What do you mean,' she asked, as they walked from the inn, 'not yet?'

He smiled, looking at the ground. 'Maybe I meant that it might slip out one day, when I'm in conversation with one of my workmates. After all, the other two were with me, weren't they? There were four of us on the island, weren't there, the boss, me, plus Jim and Bill. They're not blind, either. Not that they'd tell,' he added quickly. 'Nor would I.' His glance slid to her, slid away. 'Not intentionally.' They crossed the street, passing a row of ancient stone-built houses climbing the hill, a long terrace of them as if one supported the other.

'I'm going to my car,' she told him, 'so I'll leave you here. Thanks for the tea.' She held out her hand for the parcels, but he kept them.

'I'm going to my car, too.' They continued walking. 'Got your own car here, have you?'

'Slip of the tongue,' she told him. 'It's on loan from Miss Allen.'

'Ah, the beautiful, possessive Corinna. You've met her, then? Now you see what I meant when I told you that your Mr Cameron was out of your reach. She'll never let him go.'

'I never imagined she would.'

'So why have you followed Cameron to his home ground?' They were standing beside Corinna's red car. Lisa unlocked it and bundled all the parcels and bags on to the back seat.

'I didn't follow him, I was summoned,' she told him, emerging backwards from the car. 'I'm his secretary now. He promoted me.'

The sun-bleached eyebrows lifted into two knowing arcs. 'He did, did he? Well, well.' He smiled, but as a gesture it was reflective rather than friendly. He lifted the hand which held his car keys. 'See you up at the house in five minutes. Don't be surprised if I overtake you, will you? I'm due to see the boss on business, not pleasure.'

With that enigmatic remark, he went to his car and opened the driver's door.

Lisa spread her new clothes on the bed in her room,

admired them, then hung them in the wardrobe for the creases to disappear. That evening, she decided, she would wear the long, pleated blue skirt and a white button-through blouse.

On her desk she found enough work to keep her busy for a long time. Wondering if there was a deadline, Lisa lifted the red receiver and dialled.

'Yes?' The answer was curt, she knew, because he would have been aware at once that it was she, his secretary, calling him on the red phone.

I'll make him realise, she decided firmly, that I'm a human being, not a robot. 'I bought some nice clothes,' she told him. 'I think they'll be more suitable than the dress I wore last night.'

There was a long silence and she frowned. 'Mr Cameron?'

'Yes?' he repeated. As he spoke, there came a discreet cough from the background, followed by the clearing of a male throat. Reg Beckley making his presence known! He had probably heard every word. 'I've found your tapes on my desk. How long have I got to finish them, please?' Her voice was now brisk and entirely businesslike.

'Get as many letters as you can finished before mid-morning tomorrow.' There was a slam at the other end.

Reg Beckley was seated on the couch beside Corinna when Lisa entered the living-room. He was more formally dressed than she had ever seen him. Both pairs of eyes looked her over. Reg's thumb went up in a familiar gesture, presumably of approval, Lisa guessed, untouched by his flattery.

Corinna expressed hers verbally. 'Better, much better than the slightly démodé dress you wore last night.'

'It was the only one I had with me,' Lisa replied, wondering why the woman had to mix her praise with acid. 'I bought it for an official dinner.'

'Never apologise, never explain, as the saying goes,' Reg interposed. 'You'd look beautiful in whatever you wore, Lisa.'

Lisa sent him an irritated look, saying silently but

clearly, I don't remember giving you permission to use my first name.

Corinna glanced from one to the other. 'Have you two met before?'

Lisa rushed in, before Reg could produce one of his double-entendre comments, 'A while back now. After all, we do work for the same company, don't we, Reg?'

While she had been speaking, the door had opened. She saw with a shock that Zander stood near it, listening with a cold interest. Had Lisa's false enthusiasm for her chance connection with Reg nettled him?

Corinna, glittering in her white sequin-sprinkled closely draped dress, leaned back against the couch to gaze up at her fiancé, who now stood behind her. Her bare arms reached up for him, emphasising her attractive roundedness. He bent down so that her arms could touch his cheeks and neck above his collar-line.

Her lips puckered, inviting his kiss. Obligingly, he placed a slanted one across her mouth and she laughed, pointing. 'I've branded you with my lipstick, darling.'

Unembarrassed, he found a handkerchief and wiped it away, his eyes on Lisa. She looked away. Reg Beckley was not a fool and she knew that he, too, was watching her, probably for her reaction to Corinna's 'sex-kitten' act.

Lisa was forced to acknowledge that Corinna seemed to know every trick in the book that taught a woman how to entice a man. Which proved, Lisa mused, that Corinna's sensuality had not been put into a deep freeze when she had had that accident.

All the same, it did not add up when placed against her emotional outburst of the night before. Why had she made the shattering statement that there would be no marital relationship between Zander and herself after they were married? Why had she gone so far as to condemn her fiancé, even after he became her husband, to a life of total restraint?

Had she had someone else in mind, someone she had wanted to punish? And was that 'someone' the person who had been with her on the day of the accident?

Looking from Reg, who seemed to find his hostess's profile fascinating, to Corinna herself, she began to wonder if there had ever been anything between them.

Then a slightly cynical look flitted across his fair features and she knew for certain that there had not even been friendship. A woman with Corinna's considerable assets would not have looked twice at him. He was, after all, a mere employee of the man on whom she must, for some time before the actual engagement, have set her sights, the handsome son of the president of the company.

It was Zander who assisted his fiancée from the living room to her place at the dinner table. Lisa walked slowly behind them, with Reg beside her. Now and then he directed a look at her which said, 'Come on, look at me. I'm not as bad as you think I am.'

His hand happened to brush her arm, and she drew it away in a reflex action, looking up at him with indignation. His smile told her he had made her look at him, after all. When he gave her a large wink, she smiled, glancing away quickly.

Zander looked round as if he had eyes in the back of his head, she thought sourly. He had not missed the eye-play, as she had hoped he would.

They had almost reached the dining-room when Reg asked, casually, 'Why don't you have that operation, Corinna? You'd be back to normal then and the world—well, the fashion hounds—would be back at your feet.'

It took her a few moments to get comfortable on her chair, even assisted devotedly by her husband-to-be. Her answer to Reg's question was succinct. 'It wouldn't work.'

Lisa stole a look at Zander. He looked so handsome her heart somersaulted. But there was a remoteness about him which told Lisa that Corinna might have been more correct than she, Lisa, cared to believe about Zander's unswerving faithfulness, even within a loveless marriage.

Reg seemed determined to snap the tenuous thread of amiability which still prevailed. 'But I thought you were given every encouragement by the specialists you saw?'

He had put Corinna on the defensive and it was plainly a position she hated. 'They couldn't guarantee success, that's what they said,' she snapped in a 'now-be-quiet' tone.

'I heard otherwise,' Reg persisted, as Milly lowered her own special brand of vegetable soup in front of Corinna, then moving round the table. When she had gone, he went on, 'I heard a tale that the surgeons gave very encouraging reports of that operation.'

'You heard wrong.' There was a note of desperation in her denials now.

'Since that was nearly two years ago,' Reg persisted, 'things might have got even better. Medical science can take giant leaps these days, thanks to the medical researchers.'

Zander had finished half his soup and pushed the rest away. He hooked an arm over the back of his chair and looked impassive. Lisa's probing eyes, as she gazed at him between mouthfuls, grew certain that the nonchalance was a veneer.

He glanced up suddenly and saw her watching him. The tension between them that never went away intensified. Her eyes dropped to monitor the movements of her soup spoon as if she were engaged in a project on the subject.

'Think of it,' Reg was saying, 'you could throw away those crutches——'

'Will you leave me alone!' Corinna shouted, her hand shaking as she tried to guide her glass of water to her mouth. She put it down again. 'You have no business ... Alexander, he has no business——' Her arms reached out again, and for the second time within two days Lisa saw Corinna turn her face, sobbing, against her fiancé's chest. The woman's nervous system, she decided, hardly able to believe it, must be on a knife-edge.

'Corinna's right, Reg,' said Zander, his tone surprisingly mild, 'it's no concern of yours.'

Reg frowned, rearranging his napkin on his lap. 'No, boss. Except,' it seemed he just had to say it, 'I hate to see a beautiful woman go to waste in this ugly world.'

Lisa glanced at him with some surprise. Under his worldly cynicism, there seemed after all to be a layer of humanity.

After dinner, Zander told Reg he wanted him in his office. 'We'll continue our discussion,' Zander told him. Reg, back to normal, clicked his heels and saluted, adding an impudent, 'Okay, boss.' Zander allowed himself a smile, but it was not free from strain. Were Corinna's emotional outbursts telling on him?

As the men mounted the stairs, Corinna reclined in her special corner on the couch. Lisa tried to relax, looking forward in no way to an evening spent in her hostess's company.

'I hate that man,' Corinna confided, sipping her drink. 'He won't let a subject drop. No wonder he can't keep a woman married to him for more than two or three years!'

Lisa could see little wrong with Reg's reasoning where the operation was concerned. The wall Corinna had built around herself on that subject was for some strange reason formidable. Perhaps Reg thought that by battering away at it, he might eventually make a break-through. What puzzled Lisa so much was why he even was trying.

'Did you meet him while you were out in Lanzarote?'

The question, in its suddenness, almost tripped her up. In order to collect her wits, Lisa parried with, 'Who, Reg Beckley? I may have, but again, I wouldn't have known him, would I?'

Corinna's clear brow pleated. 'But you said earlier you'd met a while back. How long is a "while back"?'

Lisa dodged the question. 'I believe I caught sight of him at the London offices. He's tall and very fair, isn't he? Not bad looking.' She forced a laugh. 'Maybe that's why I remember him.'

Corinna lifted and dropped her elegant shoulders.

'What's his job, Miss Allen? Within the company, I mean.'

'At the moment, as far as I know, he's in charge of the whole Lanzarote project—that is, the part which Thistle International is tackling. They're just one of many contractors, or so Alexander says.'

The blonde hair swung as her head turned, first one way, then the other, an unexpected heaviness dulling the attractive eyes. They closed and her head went back, the pale hands which had once been used to frame the perfectly-shaped features lying loosely on the cushions each side of her.

Lisa watched the young woman's face, even more attractive in repose. When tears welled from under the lids, trickling down the colourless cheeks, Lisa whispered, 'Corinna, what's wrong?'

There was no answer. She had not really expected one. Moving to sit beside her, Lisa rested a hand on the slim shoulder. It was shaken off at once.

'I don't want your pity,' Corinna muttered, her throat full of tears.

Lisa found the hand bell and rang it. It was answered by Edgar about three seconds later. Gesturing to Corinna, she asked, 'Would you please ask Mr Cameron to come quickly?'

Edgar lifted a hand and was gone. Corinna said irritably, 'There was no need. He's not the one I——'

Zander entered, looking straight at Lisa. 'Something wrong?'

Lisa directed his attention to Corinna. He strode round the couch, sat beside her and gathered the sobbing form into his arms. His lips pressed against the clear forehead, his hand stroked the silky blonde hair.

Corinna's arms lifted to cling to the solidity and strength of her fiancé. 'You're so good, Alexander, so good. I want you to know how much I——'

Lisa stood quickly and Zander's eyes lifted to rest inscrutably on her face. It was no use, she couldn't stand hearing another woman telling a man she herself loved how much she loved him. Murmuring, 'Please excuse me,' she hurried out.

CHAPTER NINE

HER feet took her up the stairs, along the corridor and into her office. She had dismissed the comforts of her bedroom. There she would look inward, finding unhappiness and no solutions to the questions which slammed like hailstones against her mind.

Work was, or so they said, an anodyne in times of trouble, so she had decided to continue typing those letters which Zander had demanded by mid-morning next day. One typed letter later, there was a creak of her door.

Swinging round, she had to quieten her leaping heart. Her disappointment must have been obvious, since the man who entered said,

'No, it's not the man you fancy above every other.'

Incensed, Lisa swung back to her work. 'I know where Mr Cameron is.'

'So you're still eating your heart out for him. You won't take my advice and forget him, will you? What happened downstairs? I haven't seen him move so fast since——' He went to the window, walked back.

'Since when?'

Reg shrugged. 'Since he heard about Corinna's accident.'

'You mean, he wasn't the one who was with her when it happened?'

'What do you know about it?' His evasion of her question made her wonder whether he had been the man after all. Had he ridden away and left Corinna lying there? Lisa had sensed a suppressed resentment in Corinna towards him since he had appeared at the house.

'Only what Corinna told me,' she answered, 'and those were the bare details, nothing more.'

Should she probe more gently? 'Reg, who was with her that day?'

149

He did not answer, and this again confirmed her suspicions. He smiled to himself, sat across the room in a visitors' chair and raked in a pocket, drawing out a photographic wallet. Interested now, Lisa watched. He took a handful of pictures from it, replaced the wallet, then began to shuffle through the colour photographs as if they were a pack of cards.

'Come dancing with me tonight?' he invited casually, without looking at her. He continued playing with the pictures, sometimes altering their positions in the pack.

'No, thank you.' The idea of going anywhere with him appalled her—not that he was unattractive. It was just the air about him of being not quite trustworthy and honest. That apart, she told herself, rolling a sheet of company paper into the typewriter, there was no man she wanted to go out with except Zander Cameron, so she would stay at home.

Reg was unabashed by her refusal. 'How long since you've dined and danced? Not since your holiday, I'll bet. Not since the boss made you his girl-friend, strictly temporary, of course. His sweet little holiday pick-up.'

Her palm slammed the desk. 'I could get you fired for that!'

'Could you? You're that well in with him, are you?' He stood up slowly and strolled to her side. Again, as if they were playing cards, he dealt the photographs in a row on the desk top. He held one back.

'Where did you get those?' asked Lisa, worried now.

'From the negatives, where else?'

'Did Zander give them to you?'

'Do you really think he would? I found them in his desk drawer at the London office—the negatives, not the pictures. He's probably got those locked away in a strongbox, in case some unsuitable person gets hold of them.'

'Like you.' Her lips were dry with a growing fear.

'Like me.'

'Well, I've got a set, too. So that cancels these out, doesn't it?' When she looked up at him, he just smiled. She did not like his smile. Uneasily, she looked at the row of photographs again. 'There's one missing.'

'This?' He held it away from her, but she could see it clearly. It was, as she had known, the most incriminating of all, the picture taken by Reg himself. She was laughing up at Zander, clutching him, and she could feel the magic of him all over again. Zander's arms were around her so tightly it was a wonder she had been able to breathe. He was smiling down at her as though he had possessed her utterly. At that moment, it was difficult to breathe, too.

She tried minimising their importance. 'They're just happy holiday photos, aren't they? Can I——' she reached up, 'can I see that one more closely?'

'Oh no, Lisa Maynard, you don't catch me out like that.' He collected the others into a pile and added the ace in the pack to it. 'Come out with me and I'll forget these pictures.'

'If I don't?'

'I'll show them to Corinna. Then I'll start a tale climbing the company grapevine and produce the evidence whenever I'm called on to do so.'

'You know what you are?' Lisa muttered, between her teeth, 'a——'

'Blackmailer. I've said it for you. Now, will you come out with me tonight?'

'No. Nor any other——' He paused in the act of putting the photographs away. Lisa stared at him, her fury increasing.

'I don't believe what you threatened to do.'

'No?' His expression turned unpleasant and he moved towards the door. 'Did you say Corinna's in the living-room?'

'Zander's with her. She's in a distressed state.' It was a feeble attempt to distract him, and it failed.

'All the better. In a few minutes she'll be in an even more distressed state.'

Lisa swung on her chair to face him. 'You win. I'll come out with you. But not tonight. I must get through these letters.'

Smiling, he put away the pictures. 'Tomorrow night. I'll pick you up at seven. Okay?'

'Seven. Now please get out of here and let me get on

with my work.' Lisa looked round to make certain that
he did, in fact, go and caught a glimpse of his self-
congratulatory smile.

As her eyes returned to her work, she noticed that the
door into Zander's office had not been completely
closed. Even as she experienced dismay at the discovery,
it was opened and he came in. How long had he been in
his office and what had he heard?

He walked across to stand beside her. This desk, she
thought in a feverish effort to joke herself out of her
apprehension, must have magnetic properties built in to
it. First, Reg Beckley came to stand just there, now
Zander . . .

His mouth was forbidding, his hair falling across the
deep grooves of his frown without hiding it. It must
have taken some effort on his part, Lisa considered,
trying desperately to be sarcastic, to calm his distraught
fiancée. If I hadn't known it would have been
completely impracticable, she thought, I'd have guessed
he'd been tumbling her on the thick pile of the carpet.

It had been a joke, but it failed to raise even a spark
of amusement inside her. As she tried to concentrate on
typing a letter, she felt as if he were actually touching
her, the destructive anger raying from Zander's body.

He jerked her chin round so that she was looking
into his furious eyes. 'Do you think that getting
intimate with Reg Beckley will make you forget me?'

Her neck was hurting under the strain he was forcing
on it. 'I'm certainly not getting intimate with him. I'm
not even getting friendly.'

'So what would you call making a date with him?
Arranging a rendezvous for a deep intellectual
discussion?'

Her hand grasped his arm and forced it from its hold.
'All right,' she was rubbing her strained neck muscles,
'so I am beginning to get friendly. Maybe,' her lower
lip curled round her upper one as she recalled Zander's
tenderness towards Corinna when he had raced down
to comfort her, 'maybe I am on the way to—to
something more intimate.'

She thought he was going to hit her. Instead, he

swooped and spun her chair to face him, gripping her
under the armpits and dragging her to her feet. He
shook her until she was limp and her hair hung down
over her face. 'You do that, my two-timing lassie, and
I'll shatter your heart and crush it under my feet!'

She was pale now, feeling weak, longing for the
strength of him to hold her as it had cradled Corinna.
But there was no such fortune awaiting her. It was
necessary to fight him, tooth and nail, the more so
because she loved him with a love that knew no limits.

'You might pay me my salary and give me orders
during working hours, but there your authority over me
ends, do you understand?' He had not let her go and his
grip had tightened at every rebellious word. When he
released her unexpectedly, she staggered backwards to
her chair.

'Go ahead and ruin your life with that womaniser,'
he gritted. 'He's good at his work but at living and
loving, he's lousy. And I'll tell you this.' He stood, fists
on hips, legs apart, at the other side of her desk. 'He'll
not only destroy your innocence, and I mean destroy,
he'll turn you into any man's plaything. After he's
kicked you around for a few months, and I do choose
my words with care, even if you were to come crawling
to me for pity, I'd throw you out like the female
garbage you'd become.'

He went to the window and stared out at the near-
darkness. Utterly defeated, Lisa rested her head on her
arms on the desk. It was a few minutes later that she
felt him near her. Again, his hands were lifting her, but
so differently this time.

Now she was where earlier she had wanted to be,
wrapped about with his arms, her head against his
chest, the drumming beneath her ear telling her the
state of his emotions.

'My love, what do I do about you, my wee thing, my
girl with the laughter gone from her eyes?'

'Nothing—there's nothing you or anyone else can
do.' Her voice was thick and muffled. 'You're
engaged, you're going to be married. It's not as if
your fiancée were an ordinary, able-bodied woman.

Nothing, *nothing* must happen to make her doubt your integrity.'

She indicated that she wanted him to let her go and he released her. Sitting in her chair, she smiled up at him through the few tears she had allowed to emerge. 'You seem to be fated this evening to calming highly emotional women!'

His response was to bend, lift her chin and say, 'Smile again. At least give me that pleasure.'

She smiled and he kissed it, just as he had on the island. 'Another for your stamp book of smiles?' she tried to joke,

He smiled in response, then abruptly left.

When Reg Beckley arrived to collect her next day at the time arranged, only Corinna was present to watch them leave.

'I envy you,' she told Lisa. 'Once I danced until three in the morning, and then I only stopped because my partner——' she looked at Reg then looked away, 'wasn't capable of lifting his feet from the ground.'

Reg said nothing. Instead, he turned to Lisa and placed a kiss on her startled mouth. Corinna looked from one to the other, then as if losing interest, returned to reading the magazine on her lap.

As Lisa walked with Reg along the hall and outside to Reg's car, she saw no sign of Zander, yet she felt he was everywhere. At some window, he must have been watching them, she could sense it. And she knew what he must have been thinking of her, too.

Reg had been driving for some while before he commented, 'You're not with me. I didn't take you out for the evening to be frozen out. Come on,' his hand squeezed her thigh and she slapped it away, 'let yourself go. And if you do that again, you'll make me very annoyed, Lisa.' The words held a threat that sickened her.

'You blackmailed me here, so I'm here. You can't turn me into a sparkling companion by flashing those photographs in front of my eyes.'

He laughed. 'When there's some liquid inside you, you'll brighten up.'

They went into the countryside and Lisa tried her best to transport herself to the distant hills, imagining that she was walking among the sheep grazing in the evening sun.

The hotel's restaurant had jutting walls of Cotswold stone, in between which tables of polished wood were arranged. The ceiling was low, the lighting coming from wall brackets in which imitation candles shone with wax-free light. Lisa wished with all her heart that it was Zander sitting across the table from her.

Afterwards, there was dancing in a room from which furniture had been cleared and where there was an ancient open fireplace. A fire basket stood in its centre arranged with logs. In the winter, Lisa guessed, that fire would roar with warmth and brightness.

It was with the greatest self-control that she tolerated the feel of Reg Beckley as she danced with him. Amused, he smiled down at her.

'You really do hate all this, don't you? Well, I'm telling you something else you won't like. Tomorrow evening you're coming out with me again.'

The ready negative was poised on her lips, but she swallowed it down, making herself smile. 'Same time, same place. And who said I didn't like it?'

He seemed pleased, having taken her babbling as the result of an excess of alcohol. She had, in fact, drunk more than usual, since it was the only way she knew to get her through the long evening. At around ten-thirty, she made her muscles go loose, as if she were dropping with fatigue.

'Hey, don't go to sleep on me! You've a long, long way to go tonight, before we say goodnight to each other. And don't pretend you don't know what I mean.'

'I want to go back, Reg.' Her words were faintly slurred, both with fatigue and an unaccustomed amount of alcohol. 'I've come out with you as you said. If you don't take me straight back, I won't repeat the exercise tomorrow night.'

He grabbed her dress and his eyes took on a menace that frightened her. 'Get your things and we'll be on our way.' He let her go and she shrugged her short-sleeved, black dress into place.

He drove in silence for some time. Relieved that his mind seemed to be entirely on driving through the narrow country roads, Lisa relaxed and rested back her head.

When she felt a hand push away the jacket she had swung around her shoulders, she surfaced, startled, and realised she must have dropped to sleep. A face hovered near hers and she turned her head to try to see where they were. Reg had pulled off the road and there was nothing to see but the night's blackness. And the menace of the purpose in Reg's eyes.

Zander's words came back to her with some force, and she knew he had been right. Forcing herself to stay calm, she smiled placatingly. 'I'm tired, Reg. Sorry, nothing more for you tonight.'

'You've had a sleep, which means you must be rested. Why else do you think I let you rest for so long?'

For so long? That could only mean they were not all that far from their destination. If necessary, really necessary, although the thought of walking even a short distance alone in the darkness frightened her, she could reach Zander's house without Reg's help. Impatient now, his lips found hers, but she tried her utmost to repulse his kiss. She twisted and turned so much that he took two handfuls of her hair, stilling her movements.

His hand pulled at the high, rounded neckline of her dress. She nearly cried with relief that the back zip held. Then she heard the sound of tearing and, in her frenzy, tore her mouth from his.

'If Zander's there when I go in and he sees my torn dress——'

He let her go ill-temperedly. 'You win—tonight. Tomorrow you'll come out with me again. If you don't,' his voice threatened in the darkness, 'you know those little tricks I have up my sleeve.'

Only too thankful to have escaped him for a few more hours, Lisa answered, 'Tomorrow night,' and stayed silent for the rest of the way. When he drew up in the drive she was so anxious to get out of the car she stepped on to the gravel, and gasped with pain. In her struggles, her sandals must have come off. He threw one out and she grabbed the other. He drove away in a cloud of dust.

Lisa put on the one sandal she had, then searched in the bushes. Reg had thrown the sandal with some force. Without a torch, she knew it would be impossible to find it. Angry now, with Reg Beckley and, most of all, with herself for having submitted to his blackmail, she limped indoors, wincing at every other step.

Even though she closed the heavy entrance door as quietly as she could, it creaked and clicked loudly. Outside the living-room door, she paused, listening intently to check on whether it was empty.

There was the sound of snatched kisses, a sigh followed by Corinna's voice saying, 'Zander, for your sake I think I should have that operation. If I'm to be your wife, it's only fair to behave as a real wife should. Maybe I'll even *want* you to love me.'

Lisa frowned at the strange statement. She heard another sigh, some movement like a reaching up of arms, then the end of a lingering kiss. Sickened by the pictures her imagination was conjuring up, she half-turned, stood on the one foot that was covered by a sandal and overbalanced.

In her need to hold on to something to steady her, she grabbed the door edge, and under her weight it moved slowly open, revealing her presence to her astonished audience.

Corinna was stretched across the couch, while Zander occupied one corner. Her head was in his arms and his face bore signs of smudged lipstick. As if he was conscious of the fact, he extracted a handkerchief and rubbed his mouth.

It was then, when a pain like a bullet hitting her at the sight nearly made her double up, that she saw the contempt in Zander's face.

'Good grief,' Corinna exclaimed with amusement, 'what has he done to you? Rolled you around in a field and then raped you? You should see yourself!'

'Get out!' Zander's voice was low and furious,

flicking like a whip at Lisa's raw sensibilities. 'And stay out!'

Lisa turned, slamming the door and limping up the stairs, scarcely able to contain her tears. If he knew . . . if only she could tell him to what she had been forced to submit herself in order to save him, his precious fiancée and his internationally respected company from the stain of scandal.

Reaching her room, she threw the remaining sandal from her and sank despairingly to the bed.

Lisa rose early, having slept little. She had been pushed into a corner by the relentless course of events. Since she was no high-powered manipulator, but just a straightforward, honest young woman, they were events over which she could exercise no control.

Food did not appeal, nor did the prospect of facing Corinna or even Zander over the breakfast table. Calling into the kitchen to ask Milly for a cup of coffee, she was presented with a tray of toast triangles and marmalade, plus a whole pot of coffee.

Looking at it, Lisa laughed and shook her head, saying she could not possibly manage all that. Milly contradicted her in the nicest possible way and told her she could not work until lunchtime with no food inside her.

As she alternately typed and chewed, drank and typed, she felt her normal energy returning, plus an ability to face up to the coming evening's battle. She would go out with Reg. There was no way out of that, but this time, knowing what to expect, she would put up a fight that would leave him scarred for a long time to come.

It was as she put the empty tray aside that she heard Zander's door crash open and slam shut. She covered her ears, bracing herself for the call she knew would come. Two minutes later he buzzed her. He had not even called her on the intercom. His mood must really be black, she thought, bracing herself, opening his door and entering, head high.

His look, she knew in advance, would be reducing.

The fight was starting already, not just this evening as she had anticipated. He looked her over as if she had been brought in off the streets. A twisting pain was making its way unrelentingly upwards, causing her heart to pound in fear.

If she looked tired, as the mirror had faithfully revealed to her, then he surely must have had a sleepless night. His brown eyes blazed from black shadows placed there by failure to indulge fatigue. His cheeks and chin were still rough as if he had given them the most cursory of shaves. He was tieless and jacketless, his pale blue shirt crumpled.

He held out a handful of tapes. Lisa looked at them, startled. He surely could not have dictated those before breakfast, since there were so many.

'When you can't sleep, Miss Maynard,' his hard voice prodded, 'as it seems you could not any more than I, work is the best thing invented to take your mind off the fact.'

'You actually dictated all this in the night?'

'I did. Besides the letters I've answered, there are a couple of long reports. I shall want the work finished by the time I return this evening.'

Feeling as she did, Lisa was appalled at the thought of all that work ahead of her. 'You're going somewhere?'

'To London. Didn't Shirley tell you?'

'She did, but she told me that she used to go with you.'

He was unbuttoning his shirt preparatory, she assumed, to changing it. Fascinated, she watched his body slowly being revealed, the chest hair against which, in Lanzarote, she had nestled, the flat stomach she had so admired when they had spent that afternoon on the hotel's private beach.

Reaching his hips and the tautness of his old jeans over his thighs, her eyes lifted swiftly, as if conscious of trespassing. 'You know more about men now, Miss Maynard,' he sneered, 'after the eventful evening you spent with Reg Beckley. I'd like to bet he taught you a few tricks you didn't even know existed.'

His formality distanced them even farther from each other. It was almost unbearable after his former tenderness, the kisses and the laughter they had shared. Hadn't he warned her that she wouldn't like the man beneath the beard? How many times had he told her so?

Lisa shook her head at his statement. What was the use of denying his accusation and innuendo? 'Shall I change to go with you to the London office, Mr Cameron? I shall have to bring those tapes with me.'

'I won't need you in London. There are plenty of reliable young women I can call on to do my work.'

'Will you be training one of them, Mr Cameron, so that eventually she can take over my work completely? After you've sacked me, of course.'

He came round the desk and seized her arms, gripping until she cried out, 'Please stop!'

When he jerked her against him, she felt the roughness of his chest through her thin white blouse. His breath fanned her lips, and her head went back in a vain attempt to escape the effect on her reflexes of the feel of him and the aroma of his maleness.

'Sarcasm from you after an evening in the arms of Reg Beckley stings me about as much as a piece of dry cotton wool.' He let her go, watching her reel back with a stare of grim satisfaction. 'It might come as a shock to you to know that I do have it in mind to train another young woman to do my work. Eventually, you won't be needed here.'

Holding the tapes with both hands, Lisa cried, in an effort to hide the devastating blow he had just handed out, 'Why did you move me from my original position, then? I was happy in Personnel, far happier than I've been here, working for you. If you only meant this as a temporary appointment for me, you should have told me at the start.'

Cold derision took the place of his anger. 'I had intended it to be a permanent position. For some strange reason I can't now recall,' his eyes told her the reason if his lips did not, 'I wanted you—near.' He returned to the desk. 'After last night and your evening of what must have been near-debauchery—judging by your appearance when you came in—I don't want you near me any more.'

He pulled open a drawer and withdrew a sandal. 'Yours, I imagine? Edgar found it in the bushes this morning. I won't ask how it got there.'

'I'll tell you,' she retorted, taking the sandal. 'Reg *threw* it at me.' She added, with venom, 'Out of frustration.'

'I'm sorry for him,' answered Zander cynically. 'Maybe he didn't realise you were innocent until it was too late. Never mind, next time maybe you'll improve on your performance.'

Lisa drew her lips back. 'I hate you, Zander Cameron!' He gazed steadily at her. 'And to think that when I first met you, in Lanzarote, I actually thought I loved you.' Her voice was so low she wondered if he could hear.

He made a faint movement, then checked himself. His expression showed no mercy.

At the door, she made a final attempt to vindicate herself. 'You don't understand, Zander, you just don't understand.' If he had heard the break in her voice, he did not show it.

The day crawled by. Lisa worked continuously, determined to finish on time the typing he had given her. She even had her meals in her office, partly to save precious minutes, and partly to avoid contact with Corinna. Today, she had no reserves of energy with which to counter the other woman's sarcasm about the rough evening she was supposed to have spent with Reg Beckley.

By the time Zander walked into his office early that evening, she had finished the work he had given her. Far from adding to his fatigue, the day's work seemed to have invigorated him. Lisa had gone to him immediately the buzzer had sounded.

He gave her the briefest of glances and she knew he could not have overlooked the fact that her tiredness and paleness had persisted rather than decreased. He made an irritable come-on motion with his hand and although she felt her ire rising at his lack of courtesy, she complied by placing the pile of typed sheets in front of him.

With a wave of his hand he dismissed her. This, she decided, she could not, would not take. 'Did you find yourself a new personal assistant, Mr Cameron?' she dared. He looked up, his face expressionless and remote. 'Will you be making more frequent visits to London to train her, so that you can rid yourself of my presence all the sooner?'

She cursed herself for allowing her lower lip to tremble, but saw by his hard, piercing look that her unhappiness seemed to have made no impression on him.

'Get yourself and your sarcasm out of here,' he grated, 'before I do something I'll regret for the rest of my life!'

'That you'll never do, Mr Cameron.' Her misery was driving her on. 'Shall I quote? "Know prudent cautious self-control is wisdom's root." You quoted that at me once, didn't you, Mr Cameron? Or have you forgotten the time you—you shared my bed?' Her voice was thick now, but she would not give way in front of him.

He was round the desk in two seconds, hands on her throat, eyes on fire, his body rigid. She wanted his arms around her lovingly, not his hands grasping in rage.

Whispering, her eyes filling, she quoted Robert Burns again, ' "Should auld acquaintance be forgot and never brought to mind?" '

Zander's expression underwent a subtle change, but it did not soften. He let her go, dropping into his chair, clasping his hands on the pile of papers, waiting until she had gone.

As soon as the working day was over, Lisa gathered her things and left the office. She had received no further summons from her employer. Before going to her room, she descended the wide staircase to the living-room, guessing that Zander would not be there.

Corinna was, as usual, in her corner on the couch. She glanced up from her magazine, greeting Lisa with a frown mixed with a derisive smile. 'My goodness, you look a mess! He really did take it out of you, did Reg. If he did that to his ex-wives, no wonder they divorced him!'

Lisa did not answer the taunts. 'I'd be glad if you'd tell Milly I won't be in to dinner.'

'Tell her yourself,' was Corinna's impolite reply. Starting to read the magazine again, she looked up. 'Got a date with Reg tonight, too? Good grief, you must be a glutton for punishment!'

There was, Lisa decided, a limit to her ability to take insults. 'Would you have an inside knowledge, Miss Allen, of how Reg Beckley behaves when he's out with a woman?'

Corinna went so white with rage, Lisa felt compelled to apologise. This she did, but it did not take away the girl's indignant fury. As calmly as she could, Lisa withdrew, then ran to the kitchen as if it were a kind of sanctuary.

'I'm sorry, Milly, but I've upset Miss Allen. I couldn't help it—she provoked me so much.'

'I'm not surprised you had a bit of your own back, Miss Lisa. At times Miss Corinna's enough to try the patience of an angel. But she's got a lot to put up with, so we have to go along with her. Don't worry, I'll pop in and see if she's all right.'

'Thanks, Milly. I was going to tell you I won't be in to dinner tonight.'

'Going out, are you? Well, enjoy yourself.' Milly made her way to the living-room, following Lisa, who turned towards the stairs. 'Ah, here's Mr Alex,' Milly exclaimed, looking up. 'He'll keep an eye on Miss Corinna.' She went back to the kitchen.

Zander reached the foot of the stairs as Lisa trod on the bottom stair. His hand shot out and caught her wrist. 'What was that all about?'

'I said something to Miss Allen that seemed to upset her. She went quite white, so I told Milly, in case Miss Allen did something silly like trying to walk without help. To follow me, I mean, and scratch my face.'

Zander released her wrist and put out a hand to open the door. Taking courage from the fact that he did not seem as annoyed with her as she had anticipated, Lisa asked on impulse,

'There wouldn't have been anything between her and Reg Beckley in the past, would there?'

'You're on the wrong track, Miss Maynard,' he mocked. 'Return to square one and start again.'

Slowly Lisa climbed the stairs, still talking, 'I mean, she told me that when she had her accident, there was someone with her, but she refused to tell me who that "someone" was. I thought at first that it might have been you, but she's too bitter about the whole thing for you to have been with her, because she's still engaged to you.'

'Your detective's mind has been working hard, hasn't it?'

Lisa had stopped at the platform partway up the stairs. 'Nor would you ride off and leave her lying there.' Her eyes challenged him. 'You're too *honourable*—her word. So I guessed it might have been Reg.'

'Alexander!'

His name was an urgent cry from inside the room. He went inside at speed, closing the door hard. It was, Lisa reckoned, a reprimand intended for her. Hurrying up the remaining stairs, she closed her bedroom door just as firmly.

With the intention of taking a quick shower, she unfastened her blouse and went to her clothes rail to choose a dress. The plainest, most unattractive outfit she possessed, she decided, might cool Reg Beckley's ardour, although she had little hope of its deterring him for long.

Spreading the oldest, darkest two-piece suit she possessed on the bed cover, she looked for and found the highest-buttoning, most demure blouse in her wardrobe. Taking it on its hanger to the door, she lifted it to rest on the brass hook which had been fixed there.

As she lowered her arm, she heard the pounding of feet along the landing. They stopped outside and the handle turned. Zander had come to release on to her his fury at her behaviour towards Corinna! Diving towards the bathroom, she was just too late to escape him.

He caught her bare shoulder and twisted her round to face his rage. 'So you're out for dinner again this

evening? There's no need to tell me who your date is.
This *I* will tell *you*.' His fingers slipped under her bra
straps and with them, he jerked her against him. 'I shall
do everything in my power to stop you, and I do mean
everything.'

His eyes skated all over her, although her body, far
from feeling like an ice-covered pond, had begun to
burn at the touch of him. As his statement sank in,
there was a roar in her ears as though a fire had started
in her head.

'You mustn't stop me, Zander. I *must* go out with
him.' There was a mental picture of Reg arriving, being
told she was not accompanying him, having changed
her mind. He would reach into his pocket . . .

There was a naked fury in Zander's gaze and she
began to grow frightened at the violence which lay just
beneath the surface. '*Must* go? Why? Has he got you
pregnant already?'

Lisa twisted and fought to free herself, but finding all
that happened was that she had uselessly expended
valuable energy. There was no doubt about it, she
would need to escape from this man physically—get out
of that room—before she could be certain of keeping
that date. But in that half-dressed state?

His accusation that her moral calibre had sunk so
low rang in the high-ceilinged, echoing room. 'I will not
take your insults!' she spat, feeling the shoulder straps
cutting into her every time she made a bid for freedom.
'Will you believe me when I tell you he didn't get that
far?'

'Too bad he won't have the opportunity to take care
of that angle tonight. Last night he was probably
hampered by the fact that, until he got at you, you were
inviolate.'

'I tell you,' he had her wrists now, 'he did not
succeed! Will you please, please believe me?'

'Whether I do or not is immaterial, isn't it? He has
every intention tonight of carrying on with unfinished
business as soon as he's filled you up with enough
alcohol to break down your barriers. And from my own
experience of you in your intimate dealings with a man,'

his eyes lashed out at her, scarring her self-respect, 'you're not exactly slow in begging him to take you the moment he's coaxed you into the right frame of— mind.'

Her eyes filled at his deliberate desecration of those shared moments of happiness that last night he spent on Lanzarote. 'I know you won't believe me,' she asserted, 'when I tell you that you weren't just "a man", but a "special" man. Now, please, Zander,' her voice was husky with pleading, 'will you let me get ready to keep my date?'

Her request brought his anger to the point of eruption and she felt scalded by the lava-like spilling of it all over her body. 'There's one way of preventing you from keeping that appointment with the man who seems to fascinate you to the exclusion of all others.'

He unzipped her skirt and shook her bodily out of it. His practised hand, familiar yet grown a stranger during the passing of the weeks between, found the bra fastening. When he jerked it from her, revealing her firm young breasts, she realised just what he had meant by his statement.

His arm went under her knees and he was depositing her on to the bed. His mouth knew the way around her. He had not forgotten what had pleased her in the past. Now he made full use of his foreknowledge. He sat sideways on the bed. As his hand caught and gathered her wrists and placed them above her head, his mouth took possession of the thrusting piquancy of her breasts.

'No, no, Zander.' She was whispering now, her desire to yield warring with her fear of being prevented from keeping her appointment—and its consequences.

He stretched himself beside her and, releasing her wrists, moulded the curving shape of her with ungentle movements. He was seeking not to please her, only himself. Barbaric fingers wrapped around her hips above her briefs, and she moaned as he used his hold to jerk her round to face him.

His thumbs strayed to make circles on her stomach and she knew the conflagration he had ignited by touching her with his fire would, in a few moments, engulf them both. As she opened her mouth to urge him yet again to stop, his own closed over it. Of their own volition, her arms lifted to hold him.

There was the sound of car tyres screeching to a halt outside. It sliced through Lisa's dream world into which Zander's barbarous lovemaking had taken her. With her palms she tried pushing him away. Her limbs had tensed, her muscles stiffened, holding her head away.

'You *must* listen to me,' she insisted, resting a hand on his chest and pulling agitatedly at the soft hairs under her fingers. He slapped his hand over hers, keeping it still, but she was determined now to have her say.

'I must go out with Reg, I must! Please don't ask me why——'

There was the heavy sound of metal on metal as the newcomer knocked with an apparently supreme confidence on his employer's ancient entrance door. 'Oh no,' she muttered, 'and I'm not even dressed.'

Zander's hands were on her arms and he looked her over with some amusement. 'I'll say you're not!' His mood had changed to one of satisfaction at the knowledge that he was utterly in charge of her. Each time she tried to rise, he held her down. His finger flicked each pointed breast with lazy arrogance. 'Now I'm going to ask you why it's so important that you go out with one of my construction engineers.'

'Just let me go, that's all I ask. I have my reasons——'

'I'll bet you have. But I can supply what you're after from him, only much much better.' His lips were at her throat and a shiver ran through her.

Her mind was playing over to her what must be happening now in that large and beautiful living-room downstairs. Reg would be looking at his watch, pacing the floor, listening for her arrival . . .

With a tremendous jerk she broke free of Zander's hold, made for the bathroom door—but he caught her up. 'You can't stop me!' she cried. 'You mustn't stop me!'

'Can't? Mustn't?' His mouth had hardened, his eyes glittering at the imperious orders she had flung at him.

Lisa realised it had been a mistake to defy, to try to dictate to a man with his moral and physical strength, but she was in a desperate situation. He swung her round and into the bathroom, bolting the door and putting his back to it, still holding on to her arms.

The chase had rekindled his desire and his eyes were tracing a scorching path over her body. 'Now I'll make you mine,' he said, his voice dangerously low. 'Here on this floor, with the bolt across.' His hand went to his belt. 'But soon, my sweet one, you won't even want to get away from me.'

'Zander,' her head was thrown back in her effort to get away, 'you don't know what you're doing by keeping me here. If I don't go down there in about two minutes, Reg Beckley will do something that's going to affect us all, especially Corinna.'

She was free, but he had not moved from the door. Zander's arms were folded, his passion gone as though it had never been. 'Tell me,' he commanded.

Crossing her arms and holding herself, she shook her head. 'I think it will be too late now.' Her eyes lifted to his. 'The reason I went out with him last night, and agreed to go again this evening, was because he——' Should she go on? It was impossible now to stop, judging by his look of icy anger.

Lisa sat on the stool. 'He managed to get a copy of each of those photographs of us taken on Lanzarote. He tormented me with them, said he'd show them to Corinna if I didn't co-operate.'

He hit his palm with his fist. 'Blackmail! Trust Reg Beckley, with his twisted mind!'

There was a shouting outside, Edgar's voice calling, a hammering on the door. 'Mr Cameron, are you there?'

Zander slid open the bolt on the bathroom door and answered.

'It's Miss Corinna, Mr Cameron,' Edgar's agitated voice called back. 'She's in such a state! She keeps crying for you.'

'I'm on my way,' Zander answered grimly. 'Stay with her, Edgar, until I arrive.' He turned. 'You,' he addressed Lisa, 'I want with me.' He saw her look down at herself with dismay. Returning to the bathroom, he took a robe from the door hook, thrusting it at her. 'Put this on.'

'Zander, even with that I won't be decent!'

He took her arm. 'Either you put that thing on, or you'll come like that. Beckley wouldn't object, but Corinna might.'

Lisa slipped on the robe, tying it quickly. Her feet were bare, but he would not wait for her to find her mules. 'Why are you talking to me in that tone? *I* was the victim of the blackmail. I only gave in to it for your sake.'

'I'm sure you did.'

'That's unfair!' she protested. He ignored the accusation and forced her to walk beside him. At the foot of the stairs, he released her. There was the sound of sobbing interspersed with words of disbelief that Zander should do this to her.

Just before entering, Zander taunted, 'Talk yourself out of this one.'

'It takes two,' she answered sharply, pulling the robe more securely round her. 'The man in those pictures was you.'

The state of Corinna's face stunned her as she looked at the swollen-eyed, shaking figure on the couch.

'Zander,' Corinna reproached through puffy lips, 'how could you take a lover while you were away? And then,' the wide, accusing eyes swung to Lisa, 'bring her here as your *secretary*!' She spoke the word as if it were a term of abuse. 'After all your promises to me, too! How can I ever trust you again?'

Zander sat beside her and pulled her shaking form into his arms. Lisa could hardly stand the sight. Those arms had, only a few minutes ago, almost turned her into his lover!

Lisa saw the photographs scattered over the carpet as if they had been thrown into the air in disgust. Then she glared at Reg Beckley.

'Blackmailer!' Lisa cried. 'You see what you've done? I hope you're happy now!'

'I know what he's done,' Corinna intervened, lifting her head from Zander's shoulder, 'he's opened my eyes to the truth. If not for him, I would never have known what was going on between you and my fiancé.'

'You mean you're condoning Reg's blackmailing tactics?' Lisa demanded.

'I mean I'm condemning *you*. Look at you now, barely dressed! Look at how you came back from your evening with him,' pointing at Reg. 'You're nothing but an immoral little bitch. Not only that, you've got the audacity to accuse *him* of blackmail!'

'Audacity or not, Miss Allen,' Lisa replied with dignity, 'that's exactly what he was doing to me. Do you know how he got those photographs? He took the negatives from Mr——' she had so nearly called him Zander, 'Mr Cameron's office drawer.'

'Come on now, darling,' Reg moved to put his arm across Lisa's shoulder, 'you helped me get them. You were in on this with me, be honest.'

Lisa twisted free and stared her hatred at him. 'You're a lying, blackmailing——'

'Lisa!' The rebuke came sharply from Zander, whose hand was stroking his fiancée's hair.

Watching the loving gesture was more than she could stand. Tightening the robe belt, she cried, addressing Zander, 'I'm leaving! I'm dismissing myself. I hate the lot of you—I can't stand it here one hour more!'

'If you leave,' Zander's voice came slowly and with cutting clarity, 'not only will you lose the high salary I pay you, there will be no job for you anywhere in the company. What's more, if you go, he'll go, too.'

Lisa paled. 'You can't do that!'

'As chief executive, I can do what the hell I like.'

Reg's look was ugly now. 'If you fire me, Alex, I'll let the world know what I do know. And that wouldn't do Thistle International's untarnished reputation as a totally on-the-level company any good at all, would it? That one of its top directors——'

Zander put his gasping fiancée to one side and stood

up. His eyes blazed with anger, but his tone was mild. 'Don't you try flexing your blackmailing muscles on me, Reg!'

The man he addressed dropped his eyes under the intensity of his employer's. Lisa looked from one to the other, astonished. There was something she did not know, something which, she sensed, had nothing whatever to do with her.

'Zander,' Corinna's hand reached out, 'tell me that there's nothing really between you and that girl. Tell me all that,' a sweep of her hand indicated the scattered photographs, 'was just a holiday fling, before you settle down to marriage to me.'

Zander resumed his seat beside her, taking her hand. 'It was a holiday fling, Corinna.'

His fiancée sighed, lowering her head to his shoulder. 'Then I forgive you.' The smile she shot at Lisa was full of gloating triumph.

Stricken, Lisa sought Zander's eyes. A holiday affair, he'd called it—when she had told him that she loved him? He gazed steadily back at her, unmoved and plainly not remembering.

Reg turned to Lisa, started to sneer, saw her anguish and went out. As the entrance door closed after him, Lisa left Zander and his fiancée alone. There was simply nothing more to say.

CHAPTER TEN

LISA spent the evening wandering around the park-like gardens which surrounded the Cameron residence. Then she took a bath, telling herself she was revelling in the luxury of the mirror tiles and soft lighting, while blowing handfuls of foam.

When she found she was adding to the quantity of bathwater with the tears that ran of their own accord down her cheeks, she got out and towelled herself. What was the use of pretending? she asked herself. Her body was tingling, but her mind was numb.

Two hours of lying awake in her bed reversed the situation. Her body was inert, her mind dancing all over the place. Pulling on slacks and button-up blouse, she pushed her feet into sandals, swung a jacket from her shoulders and crept out into the corridor.

The bolts and locks which barred her way outside were, with a little puzzling over, soon dealt with. The door to the gardens creaked a little and she held her breath. Quickly, before anyone could stop her, she descended the steps with the aid of her small torch.

The night air held a chill and had her hugging the jacket around her. As she walked over the long, long lawn, the dew-damp grasses flicked wetly against her scantily-sandalled feet.

The sun chalet loomed, seeming larger in the blackness than when the daylight reduced it to its normal size. A glance at it was sufficient to revive the memories of Zander's savage, desperate lovemaking.

Skirting the hedge around the swimming pool, Lisa went through a latched gate which led into the woods. Her torch threw a small circle of light just ahead of her footsteps. The night scents from the trees, the bushes and damp layer of leaves were, she thought, better than the world's most exclusive perfumes.

These woods had been coaxing her into them from

the moment she had arrived, but there had been no time to spare for her to explore their mystery. Now, in the darkness, the trees stood tall and quietly waiting. Lisa looked about her, switching off her torch and putting it away. Waiting . . . for what?

A crackle of twigs behind her had her spinning round. Was she being followed? Reg Beckley, come to seek revenge? Bracing herself, she began to run. If only she had visited the woods before, she thought, her breath coming quickly, she would be familiar by now with where the paths lay.

It was unknown territory to her, but whoever was coming after her knew, it seemed, every tree root, every bush, even each patch of churned mud where horses must once have galloped. He was coming faster now, she could hear his every breath.

'No, Reg, no,' she shouted over her shoulder, 'for pity's sake, leave me alone! You've done your worst——'

A hand grabbing her jacket brought her to a palpitating stop. Refusing to give in, she let the jacket go and continued running.

'Lisa, for heaven's sake! I'm friend, not foe.' Zander caught her shoulders, spun her round. 'Didn't your reason tell you it couldn't have been Reg Beckley? How could he have got in here with all those stone walls to keep intruders out?'

Her breath was coming in deep gasps and she could only shake her head. It had taken him much less time to recover from his chase of her—but then he hadn't been mixing panic with flight from an unknown enemy.

Looking up at last, she saw that the wood had been flooded with moonlight. Gazing into his face, she strained to see his expression, but the moon had angled shadows across it. He held her arms and stared wordlessly at her uplifted features.

'Zander?' she whispered. 'Why did you follow me?'

He answered softly, his Scottish accent greatly emphasised, ' "Sleep I can get none for thinking on my dearie." '

Involuntarily, Lisa drew in her breath. At the same
moment he drew her to him, resting his cheek against
her hair. They stood that way for a long time and Lisa
found the tension falling from her like flower petals in a
summer breeze.

Her hand lifted and Zander moved his head at last.
Wonderingly, her palm ran over his unshaven cheek,
around his bristle-roughened neck and down to the
opened throat of his shirt. It was as though they were
back again on Lanzarote.

Her hand wandered to his hair, finding it ruffled. She
smoothed it from his forehead, then moved a daring
finger to the hairline behind, tracing it to his ear. His
breath was drawn in sharply.

'Sleep with me, my bonnie dearie,' he urged softly,
'here at my side with the trees as our roof and the leaves
our bed.'

His lips traced a path across her chin, skipping her
mouth and finding each eye, then the tip of her nose.
He lifted her hair from each ear, tracing a shivering
path around them with his tongue, electrifying her
senses and making her reach up and seek his mouth.

His head would not come down at her request. He
held away, laughing at her eagerness—but it was a
laugh not of mockery but of pleasure. His hands had
been busy and were invading her unbuttoned blouse.
Then it lay on the ground in the moonlight and was
joined by her bra.

Now his head bent, not to kiss but to tease her breasts,
pure white in the silver-swathed night. She did not stop
him removing her slacks. Instead, she eased his shirt from
his shoulders, resting her cheek against his chest and
holding his lean waist in the circle of her arms.

He was spreading her jacket with his foot and easing
her down until they were lying locked in each other's
arms. 'My Lisa, the misery I've been through without
you each night! I'm making you mine and to hell with
the rest of the world.'

'Zander, do you remember—no yesterdays and no
tomorrows? Only now, this minute? Remember how I
told you I loved you?'

'Do you think I could ever forget?' he growled, biting her ear and making her go cold and burning at the same time.

'And——'

He grew impatient with her talking and covered her mouth, drinking deeply of its sweetness, searching and exploring until she was almost mindless with desire. He stroked and caressed her breasts to hardness and she felt the pulsating warmth of him against her.

'Now,' he whispered, 'now, my love.' He was so gentle she could have cried. Then, their bodies throbbing in time to a rhythmic, internal drum, they were lifted to tread cloud which turned golden in the moonlight as they reached the heights together.

For a long time they lay entwined. Afterwards, Zander moved on to his side and pulled her with him. She remembered the night they had lain on the beach and the tide had crept closer until it was lapping their legs. 'Let it come in,' he had said, 'let it take us away to eternity.'

Lisa had shivered then and she shivered now. He touched her skin and felt its coolness. She held fast to him for one brief, intimate moment, and he kissed her swiftly and hard as she lifted her face from his chest.

After helping her dress, he pulled on his own clothes, then leaned back on his elbows. He stared at the swaying outlines of the treetops. His face was washed by moonlight and Lisa saw that his features held, not the happiness she had expected, but a deep, inexplicable pain.

Snuggling close, she tried to bring him back to her by curling her arms about one of his. 'I'm yours, now, Zander,' she whispered. 'Nothing can take that away.'

He turned his head and kissed away her puzzled frown. Lifting himself to his feet, he thrust his hands into his waistband and stared at the tall, outspreading shapes around them.

'So much now,' he commented flatly, 'for my being an *honourable* man!' He spoke the word as if its taste had turned sour.

Lisa scrambled to her feet and faced him. 'I don't

understand, Zander. What does it all mean? Why does Corinna refer to you as being honourable? And why was making love to me so wrong? I've made no demands on you, like asking you to break off your engagement with Corinna.'

He looked down at her broodingly. 'If I could, I would, but it's quite impossible.' He gazed at her for a long time. 'If I asked you to become my lover, would you?'

'After you're married? Oh, Zander...' Her eyes widened as the silver light turned them grey. 'No!'

He nodded as if she had given him the answer he had expected. He put out his hand as he turned to go, but Lisa shook her head, saying, 'You go in. I'll come in a moment.'

As the sound of his strides died away, she threw herself on the brittle leaf-layer and let her tears mingle with the dew.

Next day, it was a torment of the most terrible kind to have to face Zander impersonally across his desk. They talked and acted as if nothing had happened between them in the small hours of the morning, but there was an interplay of eyes that told a different story.

It was mid-afternoon when Lisa said with a heavy sadness, 'Zander, I think I should leave.'

'You'll stay, do you hear?' His fist hit the desk-top. 'You'll stay!'

Lisa tensed at the revelation of a simmering anger beneath his apparent surface calm. Anger against whom, she wondered, her—or himself? In the mood he was in, she dared not argue. All the same, she had to express her own feelings.

'There's a limit to what I can take. Surely you understand that!'

His eyes raged at hers, until he saw her misery. He seemed to put his emotions on a tight rein. 'What do you think I'm feeling?'

Helplessly, she shook her head. 'Did you sleep— afterwards?'

His anger returned and his head went back, revealing

his strong, tanned throat. 'I still can't sleep without you. So,' his shoulders lifted and fell, 'I'll spend the rest of my life not sleeping.'

Aghast at his attitude, she whispered, 'Have you considered how I feel, will feel for the rest of my life?'

'You? You'll forget me in time. You said it yourself towards the end of our first—acquaintance.'

'I didn't mean it. I only said it to comfort you. Just as I tried to comfort you last night.'

'That's a new name for it,' he said with cutting cynicism.

She let it pass, knowing it was useless even trying to reason with him. 'I'll never forget you,' she declared with a deep sincerity.

'If I were you, I'd make it my business to forget me. Otherwise, I'm sorry for your husband.'

'How could you? How could you speak to me like that, after all that happened last night?' She turned to leave him, but he was out of his chair and swinging her to face him.

His hands caught her hips and pulled her against him. Her arms reached up and locked round his neck, while her cheek found a place over the hammering of his heart. 'Zander, oh, Zander!' All her distress was in the words.

He held her away, 'Lisa mine,' he said raggedly, and wrapped her in his arms.

Her body was aching for him, and already, in answer to his powerfully stirring desire, hers was beating like a pulse gone mad all over her body. Her face lifted to his and he saw her wide, full lips curving into a smile.

It was as though a bright light shone through his eyes from his inner being. 'You've given me back your smile, my Lisa.'

She shook her head. 'You gave it back to me.'

'Then I'd better retrieve it and add it to my collection.' He caught her lips as though his intention was to swallow the smile. She welcomed his driving, possessive intrusion.

When the kissing was over, his shoulder received her resting head. Momentarily satiated, they stood in a moment's share of the deep peace which links all lovers after the merging of one into the other is over.

The sound of Milly's voice calling to Edgar brought them back to their surroundings. He returned to his desk. Lisa, without another glance at him, went back into her office, forcing herself to work on as if nothing had happened.

At dinner, Corinna flaunted her possessiveness towards her husband-to-be. For much of the meal she managed to address not a single word to Lisa who, in any case, spent most of the time avoiding her employer's eyes.

The meal was almost over when Edgar's head came round the door. 'Telephone, Mr Cameron. It's Mr Beckley for you. Urgent, he said.'

Zander nodded, remarking, 'To Reg Beckley, everything is urgent where his work's concerned. If he hadn't been such a damned good engineer, he'd have been fired long ago.'

As the door closed behind Zander, Corinna turned her gaze fully on to Lisa. 'You love Alex, don't you?' she gloated. 'I could see that from those photographs Reg showed me. Well, too bad for you! I'm the one who's going to get that man.'

'I understand that, Miss Allen,' Lisa responded levelly.

Corinna shook her head. 'You only think you do. You think it's because Alexander won't desert me because of these.' She indicated her legs.

'Yes, I do,' Lisa replied with directness.

'Carry on thinking it. It doesn't matter that,' she clicked her fingers, 'to me what you think.' She held up her engagement ring. 'Look at that beautiful emerald and those diamonds. Wouldn't you like to have that in your possession, wearing it on your engagement finger—for the man you love?'

It was not Corinna's taunting that nettled Lisa so much as being unable to hit back in the same terms. 'Emeralds are beautiful, I agree,' she answered, as if giving the matter her consideration, 'but I'd prefer a smaller setting with, maybe, a pure white diamond. That's just my taste, isn't it? That setting is yours.'

Zander erupted into the room. He went straight to Corinna, bending over her, taking her hand. 'I have to tell you something.' Her long hair swung, half-covering her face. Zander moved it gently to one side. The gesture made Lisa shut her eyes.

'Bad news?' Corinna asked, her face paling in advance of Zander's reply. Her perfectly-shaped mouth opened on a gasp and she whispered hoarsely, 'Hamish?'

It came back to Lisa ... Myra reading out the list of the company's directors. 'Mr A., Mr A., and Mr H.' Hamish the unknown figure, the younger son. The family's 'black sheep', Myra had called him.

'Car accident, late this afternoon. There was a pile-up on the motorway, going towards London. He was moving too fast to stop himself joining it.'

Corinna's free hand joined her other and they both clung to Zander's. 'Tell me now—did he survive?'

Zander nodded and Lisa would almost feel Corinna's relief. It was shortlived. 'How badly injured?'

'Extent of injuries not yet known, Reg said. Hamish was taken to the nearest hospital.'

'Was Reg with him?'

'In the rear seat. Seems Hamish had dropped some others, and was taking Reg on to the next town.'

Lisa noticed that Corinna was shaking. 'Is he conscious, Alex?'

'Drifting, apparently. Corinna, he keeps asking for you.'

Her eyes, Lisa thought, surely couldn't open wider. 'Oh dear Alex, forgive me, but I still love him. I've never stopped.'

'Do you think I don't know that, sweetie?'

She did not seem to have heard. 'I must go to him.' She tried to rise, but dropped back helplessly. 'Take me to him, Alex. I don't care what kind of physical mess he's in, now or in the future, I want to stay with him, nurse him back to health.'

'After what he did to you?'

Corinna stared up at her fiancé. 'You expect me to recoil from him like he did from me after my riding accident?' She shook her head fiercely. 'A man might do that to a woman as he did, but a woman doesn't do that to a man. Not this woman, anyway.' She looked around for her crutches.

Lisa took them to her while Zander lifted her to her feet.

Corinna's head went back proudly. 'I'm going to have that operation. What's more, it's going to succeed because I've got the will-power to make it.' She took a few painful steps, then stopped. 'I'm going to make myself just as beautiful as I was in the old days.' She stared at Lisa without really seeing her. 'You're going to see my face on magazine covers again before many months have passed!' She looked at Zander. 'If Hamish has forgotten this,' with her head, she indicated her disabled state, 'and when he comes round properly he still doesn't want me, will you still have me as your wife?'

There wasn't even a trace of hesitation as Zander answered, 'I swear I shall honour my pledge to you.'

Corinna reached up to kiss his cheek. 'You're a wonderful man!'

Helping his fiancée on her painful way, Zander spoke to Lisa over his shoulder. 'I may be away some time, depending on what happens. I'll let my parents know. Do whatever you can in my absence, will you? Leave the rest until I return.'

'Yes, Mr Cameron,' Lisa answered expressionlessly.

For a second their eyes met. His were blank, hers were empty.

A week had passed since Zander and Corinna had left. It was the longest week of Lisa's life.

Mid-week, a call was put through to her desk by Milly. Knowing it would not be Zander since it had been connected to the wrong-coloured phone, Lisa answered with a false brightness.

'You sound happy,' the caller remarked cheerfully.

'Myra! How are you? And Phil? Me, I'm fine,' she invented. 'Yes, the job's going well. No, I don't miss London, I like working in the countryside. And you?'

'Guess what?' Myra laughed. 'We're having a baby. Isn't that great?' She giggled. 'Me, I mean, not Phil. Yes, he's on top of the world. The whole office has adopted it, although it's got a long way to go yet before it makes its appearance. Got to call it "it" for now, haven't I?'

'Myra, I'm delighted,' Lisa answered, with no small twist of her heartstrings. 'You'll be leaving soon. No? Carrying on to the last minute? Yes, I believe it's the fashion.'

Having talked for a while, they rang off. The dull, empty ache which Lisa had experienced for the past few days intensified.

Sometimes, in the evening, Lisa sat with the television on but with her eyes closed. One day, Milly crept across and turned off the neglected set.

'You didn't mind me doing that, did you, Miss Lisa? Only you weren't watching and you looked so lonely.'

Lisa found a smile from somewhere. 'Do I? Sit down, Milly. Rest your feet.'

Gladly Milly complied. 'Have you ever met Hamish Cameron, Milly?' Lisa asked.

'Many times.' Milly laughed. 'He always was a young rogue.'

'Was he the person who was with Miss Allen when she had her accident?'

'He was. Hasn't anyone told you what happened?' She settled more comfortably in the chair, as if she enjoyed the role of story-teller. 'Well, Miss Corinna was engaged to Mr Hamish. She was out riding one day.'

Lisa nodded, saying that Corinna had told her that.

'Mr Hamish was with her. They were going to jump a gate,' Milly explained, 'and Mr Hamish was determined to get there first. He jostled Miss Corinna out of the way, his horse jumped the gate and he turned and waited. Well, Miss Corinna's horse was wrongly lined up for the jump, took it at the wrong angle and——'

'Slipped and fell, throwing Corinna.' Milly nodded. 'Then what happened?'

'Well, it seems that Hamish was so horrified by what he'd done, he galloped off, leaving Miss Corinna lying there all twisted and unconscious. I think he thought he'd killed her.'

Lisa frowned. 'He didn't come back to the house for help?'

Milly shook her head. 'Mr Alexander got so worried after a couple of hours, he went out looking. He's the one who found her. You know the rest, don't you?'

'No,' Lisa whispered.

'Well, Miss Corinna was in hospital for weeks. Hamish didn't go and see her once, not once. What's more, when she was brought home, and he did come when she pleaded with him on the telephone, he was so upset at the change in her, he broke off their engagement and never came near her again.'

'Then?' Lisa waited breathlessly.

'Mr Alexander was so angry with his brother, himself being such an honourable man, he asked Miss Corinna to marry him in his brother's place. She accepted. Now you surely know the rest.'

Lisa nodded and was silent.

'Can't get over it, can you? Nor can most people when they're told. Nothing will turn Mr Alexander from his set course. He'll stick to Miss Corinna through thick and thin.'

'Which is why they call him an honourable man?'

'It is, dear. And he is honourable, too, don't you ever doubt that.'

Lisa shook her head slowly.

'You've gone a bit white, dear. Would you like a nice cup of tea? It's a sad story, isn't it? But it's going to have a happy ending, mark my words.' Milly heaved herself out of the chair.

'Thank you for telling me that story, Milly.'

'It was nothing, dear. I'm surprised you didn't know it already.'

It was late, but Lisa could not settle anywhere. Bed had proved an unwelcoming place.

Walking about the room, she forced herself to a decision. Not in any circumstances, she told herself fiercely, can I go on living and working here. I love

Zander, *love* him. It would be pure hell to be near him and yet know he was Corinna's husband and out of her reach for ever. Because he was an hourable man . . .

Pulling on a jacket over her short-sleeved top and slacks, she made her way downstairs. This time Edgar heard her and came out of his and Milly's small suite.

'Where are you going this time of night, miss?' he asked, a jacket covering his pyjama top and trousers.

'For a walk, Edgar, in the grounds. I can't sleep, so I thought a walk would help me. I'll just wander around for a bit.' Edgar nodded. 'Don't worry, I'll lock up after I come in.'

'Thanks, miss,' he said. 'Make sure you shoot all the bolts, won't you?'

Lisa smiled. 'And turn all the keys.' Edgar retreated, closing the door.

It was the woods she made for, using her torch, playing it over the ground, seeking in vain for where she had lain with Zander in the early hours and made passionate, fulfilling love.

Tired at last, she walked back slowly to the house. Letting herself in and locking up as carefully as Edgar had directed, she noticed that a light was on in the entrance hall. So Edgar had come down after all, to check up that she had secured the house safely.

It was not Edgar who had turned on the light. Nor was it Edgar seated in an armchair in the living-room, head back, eyes closed, seeming tired to his very core.

Standing in the doorway, Lisa removed her old jacket and put it in a pile in the hall. Creeping across the room, she whispered, 'Zander?'

His eyes came open, his head turned and he saw her. His gaze stayed on her for so long, she wondered if he was still half in his dream. Then she noticed that his beard was growing back. Her fingers pressed against her lips as she saw the black growth of hair around his mouth, on his cheeks and chin.

The man she had first known had come back. The step she almost took towards him was checked the moment it began. His smile lightened the shadows around his eyes and his arms came open.

It was an invitation she would not, could not resist. Her hands clung to his zipped jacket which he had plainly been too tired to remove. Her face burrowed into him, inhaling his male scent, loving every part of him.

A curiously rough hand grasped her chin and turned her face to him. He murmured, ' "But to see her was to love her, Love but her and love for ever." '

'Robert Burns?' she queried, her eyes dancing. 'He loved many women, Zander.'

'And I love one.' He did not say which one.

He sat up, put her to one side and shrugged out of his jacket. He bunched it and threw it across the room, watching as it fell to the floor. Then he took her back again, on to his knee, wrapping her around and resting his hairy cheek on her upturned forehead.

'Tell me what happened, Zander,' Lisa demanded. 'How badly was your brother hurt?'

'Broken bones and so on. Nothing too serious. He'd been sensible enough to wear his safety belt which prevented him from being too badly injured.'

'Reg Beckley?'

He looked down at her, the warmth in his eyes banished. 'Why are you so curious about him?'

'Purely compassionate reasons, I assure you.'

Under her, she felt him relax. 'Reg walked out of the crash untouched. Did I ever tell you? He was not an ordinary employee. He's been a friend of Hamish's since they were boys together at school.'

'Which is why he seemed to know Corinna so well? Now I get it.'

'He nearly got you.'

She frowned, which demanding male lips immediately kissed away. 'I think that episode's best forgotten, don't you?'

'Agreed.' Zander's head went back again, his eyes closed. Lisa watched as a transforming quietness relaxed his face. She thought he was on the edge of sleep again, but he began to speak.

'Corinna is in hospital now. She's had the operation. Already the surgeon is more than hopeful that, with time, maybe a long time, she'll be walking normally again.'

Lisa's fast-beating heart began to slow down. 'Which means you'll be marrying her as soon as she's able to come home.' She had made it a statement.

Zander's eyebrows lifted. 'You're determined to marry me off to her, are you?' He smiled and his head went back again. 'I'd like to hear my brother's reaction if I took away his wife-to-be!' At Lisa's puzzled look, he added, 'They're reconciled, you foolish woman. Have I made that clear now?'

It took a few moments to sink into Lisa's brain. 'You mean——?'

'I mean——' Zander reached into his slacks pocket, 'this.' He withdrew the emerald and diamond engagement ring Corinna had been wearing and placed it on the low table next to them.

'Corinna's marrying Hamish? So you're free?'

'Free, released from my promise, able to go wherever my fancy takes me.' He looked at her with narrowed eyes that made her heart leap. 'Free to take to bed whatever woman I fancy.'

'Oh.' Lisa looked across the room. He had not got around to telling her directly, but he was trying to say she was an embarrassment to him now. 'I'll go, then.' She made to remove herself from his lap. With arms of steel, Zander held her back.

'Where were you thinking of going?'

'To bed. I couldn't sleep, so I went for a walk——'

'I'm tired, too. We'll both go to bed. My bed.'

Lisa shook her head. 'I'm sorry, Zander, but the answer's no.'

'You're turning my offer down?'

Startled, she stared at him. 'What offer?'

'Marriage. What else do you think I was talking about?'

Her head was shaking again. 'It doesn't matter, Zander. I understand your reason for suggesting it. It's true what everyone has said about you. You're a wonderful, upstanding man, honourable until it hurts. Just because we made love, you don't have to marry me.'

His muscles had been tensing under her all the time she had been speaking. Now he almost threw her from him, heaved himself upright and grabbed her shoulders.

'*Have* to marry you? I'm asking you to marry me! Obviously your poor brain is too tired to take the invitation in. So I shall have to *tell* you you're marrying me—as soon as arrangements can be made. Now do you understand?'

Her heart was in her eyes as she looked up at him. 'I understand—boss.'

Her impish reply aroused in him a love-fury. He undressed her before she knew what he was about, kissing her wherever he removed each item. She shivered, looking round. 'Not here——'

'Whose house is this?'

'Yours.'

'Ours. Now, woman of mine, remove my shirt.'

With shy hesitancy, she obeyed. Soon they were lying together on the couch and he was coaxing her, caressing her to a gasping state of arousal and longing.

'My love, my only love,' he said softly. 'I shall, indeed, love but you and love for ever.'

The fires were roaring through their bodies as they melted one into the other and, for the second time, Zander made her his own. This time, she knew he loved her as much as she loved him. This time, as the fires died down, there were no barriers to their mutual joy.

He whispered against her ear, ' "She's a lovesome wee thing, this sweet wee wife o' mine." '

Lisa pressed her forehead to his chest, then lifted her head. His arms tightened even more securely around her.

'Och, awa' wi' ye,' she declared, her voice as broadly Scottish as she could make it. Then she looked at him with shining eyes, laughing.

Harlequin Plus

A WORD ABOUT THE AUTHOR

Born in London and raised in North Essex, a county in eastern England, Lilian Peake grew to love the countryside, going for long rambling walks and filling a journal with all she observed. She became secretary to a local mystery writer, then embarked upon a career in journalism.

From fashion writer with a London magazine, she moved on to a position as advice columnist with yet another magazine, both of which jobs, she feels, contributed to a greater understanding of people.

Until almost the moment she started writing her first novel, Lilian believed that she could not do it. "Then I read a book that challenged me," she said. "I remember thinking, *I could write like that!* So I did."

Today, Lilian Peake is the wife of a college principal. Her interests vary, but reading and listening to music top the list. "And as I do the housework," she admits, "I think about my characters and my plots."

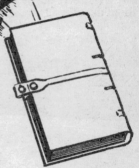

HARLEQUIN CLASSIC LIBRARY

Great old romance classics from our
early publishing lists.

FREE
BONUS
BOOK

On the following page is a coupon with
which you may order any or all of these titles.
If you order all nine, you will receive a FREE
book – *Hospital Nurse*, a heartwarming classic
romance by Lucy Agnes Hancock.

The fifteenth set
of nine novels in the
HARLEQUIN CLASSIC LIBRARY

LUCY AGNES HANCOCK
Hospital Nurse

Great old favorites...
Harlequin Classic Library

Complete and mail this coupon today!

FREE
BONUS
BOOK

Harlequin Reader Service

In U.S.A.
2504 W. Southern Avenue
Tempe, AZ 85282

In Canada
649 Ontario Street
Stratford, Ontario N5A 6W2

Please send me the following novels from the Harlequin Classic Library. I am enclosing my check or money order for $1.50 for each novel ordered, plus 75¢ to cover postage and handling. If I order all nine titles at one time, I will receive a FREE book, *Hospital Nurse*, by Lucy Agnes Hancock.

☐ 127   ☐ 130   ☐ 133
☐ 128   ☐ 131   ☐ 134
☐ 129   ☐ 132   ☐ 135

Number of novels checked @ $1.50 each = $_____
N.Y. and Ariz. residents add appropriate sales tax $_____
Postage and handling $_____.75
                                    TOTAL $_____

I enclose _____
(Please send check or money order. We cannot be responsible for cash sent through the mail.)
Prices subject to change without notice.

Name _____
            (Please Print)

Address _____
                         (Apt. no.)

City _____

State/Prov. _____

Zip/Postal Code _____

Offer expires August 31, 1984   40256000000

Get this book FREE!

Mail to:

Harlequin Reader Service

In the U.S.
2504 West Southern Avenue
Tempe, AZ 85282

In Canada
649 Ontario Street
Stratford, Ontario N5A 6W2

YES! I want to be one of the first to discover
Harlequin American Romance. Send me FREE and without
obligation *Twice in a Lifetime.* If you do not hear from me after I
have examined my FREE book, please send me the 4 new
Harlequin American Romances each month as soon as they
come off the presses. I understand that I will be billed only $2.25
for each book (total $9.00). There are no shipping or handling
charges. There is no minimum number of books that I have to
purchase. In fact, I may cancel this arrangement at any time.
Twice in a Lifetime is mine to keep as a FREE gift, even if I do not
buy any additional books.

Name   (please print)

Address   Apt. no.

City   State/Prov.   Zip/Postal Code

Signature (If under 18, parent or guardian must sign.)

154 BPA NAP7

AR-SUB-200